For Mahmoud

Chapter 1

THE RAYS of early, summer sun burst through the open windows of Siobhan's consulting room. A glass fronted fire, surrounded by brushed aluminum inserted in the wall, was the central focus. A designer feature, used more to create a sense of warmth, it alleviated the gloom of the long, dark days of Irish winters. There were no ornaments and no clutter. There were no pictures or photographs; not a sign of any large framed degrees, advertising her academic achievements in the field of psychology. The room was bare, devoid of anything other than peaceful uninterrupted calm.

This was where the victims of violence, and sometimes the perpetrators of violence, came to dump their pain, shame, guilt and misery. This was the room where people learned how to heal their fractured minds and recognize that they too, had the right to happiness and fulfillment.

The room overlooked her garden, which designed to be a place of healing and harmony. Siobhan had implicit trust in the curative powers of water, hence had built various water-features to create an easy flow of sound and motion. The garden had three small square manicured lawns surrounded by octagonal granite walkways. In summer, the lawns were used for various, alternative relaxation techniques.

'How can people heal when they don't know how to breathe?' she thought. 'When their body and mind has been battered, the only thing they know is how to hold their breath.'

In a secret part of the garden, Siobhan had placed a large, ceramic Urn behind a Sage bush. After writing down their inner-most personal thoughts of rage, sadness, and loss, her clients would tear their writings to pieces, deposit them in the Urn and burn them as a cleansing exercise. The grey smoke this process created was symbolic insofar that it carried away the dark emotions her clients had been holding onto. They were now ready to let go and move on.

As Siobhan leaned out of the open window that morning, admiring and breathing the view, the sunshine created a halo of colours around her head. These were a tribute to her visits to Nicky Clarke, the renowned London stylist, every six weeks. The weekends away were a gift to herself, from herself.

She always travelled alone. Siobhan would take the early Friday morning flight to London City Airport, and then travel to the Radisson in Covent Garden, before arriving in Clarke's salon in Mayfair. The maestro himself always greeted her. They had known each other for years. They didn't have friends in common; she had always politely refused any invitation to participate in his world.

Siobhan was her own woman; she shared nothing of her life with anyone. The exception to this self-imposed rule was her membership in 'The Three Keteers.'

During her first term at Fitzwilliam College in Cambridge, she had formed a relationship with two undergraduates, Mary and Zarah. The three women had created their own 'secret society' which had endured long after they all graduated. Their trust in each other had developed and been proven over many years, so once a year they spent at least one week together on holiday, catching up and comparing the total number of grey hairs they had acquired since they last met.

The salon was pure escapism for Siobhan. She would close her ears to the babble of women who were dissatisfied with their lives. She privately loathed gossip and second-hand information. It was easy for her to tune out the emotional, over-the-top disclosures, women made as their discolored roots faded into oblivion. But she knew that hairdressers were not bound by any ethical code of confidentiality. Discretion was not a word included in their vocabulary. The words, 'strictly between you and me,' whispered behind the back of a hand, was usually a precursor to an anonymous telephone call to a magazine of the variety which she referred to 'picture galleries.'

Siobhan loved these weekends away. When in London, she ate at the Freemasons Arms in Long Acre. Although she didn't consume alcohol, she never felt the urge to explore alcohol or chemical dependency, her pleasure at the Freemasons was the establishment's sausage and mash and tourist-watching. Everyone knew her there. It was a home away from home.

Linda, the pub's landlady, had almost completed a pre-counseling course and developed her own theoretical perception of what she termed 'pubology.' The establishment's staff were all beneficiaries of a 'pubology certificate' accredited, designed and run off Linda's computer.

Recipients of the award were required to have the ability to deal with 30 Japanese, bowing over British Fish and Chips, without mentioning the attack on Pearl Harbor. Recipients were also trained not to mention Adolf Hitler whilst serving Shepherd's Pie to Germans, or be discourteous to George W Bush, certainly within hearing distance of American diners.

Siobhan didn't shop in London. Window shopping was also an anathema to her as it had no point or purpose. Dublin provided all her requirements in that area which she usually limited to Karen Millen. Instead her afternoons in London were spent walking by the Thames or visiting museums or art exhibitions. Her evenings were spent at the ballet, theatre or the Royal Opera House.

Covent Garden re-energized her body and mind. It was her special time, and as far as she was concerned, she deserved it. She needed it. There was a time when she worked continuously but had suffered a burn out. A week in Provence with Mary and Zarah had cured her. At the time, her body had ceased functioning. She had almost convinced herself she had a brain tumor, or an invisible hatchet buried in her head. Siobhan had learned the hard way that commitment to 'self-responsibility' takes priority over everything else.

Now breathing in the healing scent of Lavender, she felt a surge of pride in creating her own private haven of peace and tranquility from a piece of land which no one had wanted. She looked at her watch, 6.20a.m. Her first client would soon arrive.

Siobhan's early morning clients were usually self-employed, or top executives. The majority of them workaholics, who could survive on four hours sleep a night. They didn't consult her because they were addicted to their work, in fact they enjoyed and craved for more. They didn't have time to enjoy the financial benefits of their addiction; in fact they only enjoyed their achievements for the seconds it took them to recognize they had achieved, before moving onto their next target.

Siobhan had no desire to change their way of life, her only desire was the successful outcome of enabling them to solve a problem, which inhibited them working at the speed they insisted to work. These were what she termed as her 'bread and butter clients.'

They paid the highest fees, which gave her the opportunity to do more Pro-Bono work for the less well off in society. This was the work which lit a fire in her belly.

The crash of the Celtic Tiger had made the marginally poor, poorer. The mildly, economically depressed, chronically depressed. Weak relationships became weaker; addictions became stronger, as more and more people lived under the threat of redundancy. Missed mortgage repayments resulted in homelessness and the steady destruction of the family unit, suicide became more frequent.

A black Ferrari turned into the drive. 'Thank God for that,' Siobhan said to herself: 'it will be an easy session.'

Ferrari Allan, or Harley Davidson Allan, was the same person with separate attitudes.

He didn't have a split personality. He recognized he had choices and this was how he chose to live. Harley Davidson Allan was a risk-taker who didn't know how to control the risks. Swathed in leathers as soft as chamois, he was aggressive, obnoxious and a sexual predator; trawling the European, seedy nightclubs and bars to pick up as he called it 'a piece of filth.'

He wasn't fussy about the gender of his piece of filth; he considered his bisexual desires quite normal. The man who stepped out of the car might have been every woman's dream but he belonged only to himself.

Six foot three and in prime physical condition, his strawberry blonde hair unadorned by sprays, waxes or gels enabled his habit of sliding his fingers through his hair without any disruption.

His midnight blue Hugo Boss suit, impeccable over a brilliant white Cannali shirt. The only colours he ever deviated from were in his silk YSL ties. His shoes were hand-made in Italy. Summer or winter he wore socks made from the finest, almost transparent silk. Siobhan waited one minute before responding to the soft chime of the door.

Walking straight past her he smiled, 'Good morning Siobhan, how are you today?'

'I'm fine thank you Allan, how are you?'

Shrugging off his jacket, he sat in the chair and looked her straight in the eyes, 'I'm well, thanks, really well.'

The fragrance of Cartier Eau de Toilette wafted across the scent of Lavender.

'He walked into a room, and in seconds owns it,' she thought. 'The epitome of power, wealth and self-confidence.'

'I've just arrived from Moscow, cut another two minutes off our time Siobhan, did it in three hours 25 minutes.'

Siobhan recognized this was part of a game Allan played, constantly challenging himself. He owned a Gulf Stream G45 Jet and his own helicopter. He had a pilot's license, but rarely used it, preferring instead to employ pilots and use his time working.

The private jet was simply another tool for Allan; he didn't have time for airports. His domicile was Zurich - no double taxation and most of his business was done off-shore.

He had made trillions for his clients managing their portfolios and millions for himself. He was an analytical genius. Home in Dublin was a permanent suite in the Merrion Hotel, in London Claridges, Paris the Ritz and in New York the Four Seasons.

He had recommended Siobhan to many of his wealthy clients. Her answer was always the same.

'I don't do private jets, hotel suites or palaces. They can make an appointment the same as everyone else and if I have a space they can come here, the same as everyone else.'

There had been the odd 'face' as she put it, but she found the entourage of bodyguards and Limo's irritating.

'You know Siobhan,' Allan said, 'every time I go to Moscow I seem to develop an obsession with dirt. I must wash my hands fifty times a day. For instance today after we were airborne, I stripped off all my clothes, including my shoes. Put everything in a bin-bag, tied it with two knots to seal it, showered, and put on all new clothes. What the hell is all that about Siobhan? I hope I'm not going down the same weird road as Howard Hughes!'

Siobhan looked at Allan taking in his blue questioning eyes, his perfect white teeth and manicured hands.

'What hotel do you stay in, in Moscow?'

'The Ritz Carlton,' he replied.

'Is it cluttered?'

Allan looked out of the window, a slight frown marking the space between his eye brows.

'It is a bit, mostly with flowers. Huge vases every-where. Really over the top and unnecessary,' he paused.

'Yes, come to think of it, it's not as minimalist as I like. There are so many paintings on the walls by local artists, they almost look like wallpaper. Do you think that's the problem Siobhan?'

Siobhan, concentrating on Allan's expectation of her solving this problem.

'It could be Allan, you hate clutter, you believe clutter makes chaos and chaos affects your thinking and concentration.'

Allan relaxed back into his chair and took a deep breath, 'You could be right Siobhan, I'll change the hotel and see if I feel different on my next trip.'

They sat opposite each other in comfortable silence. Siobhan, waited. Used to these barren episodes, she knew Allan would speak when he felt the necessity.

Allan's concentration drifted from the excitement and achievement of cutting two minutes off his flight-time, to admiring the length of Siobhan's legs. He could never understand how it was possible to have such long, elegant legs but small, dainty feet.

His admiration for this beautiful woman in front of him surpassed any fantasy he had of the female species. It wasn't just the packaging. Women can reinvent themselves if they have the money, was his point of view.

'It's her integrity,' he explained to his father, not long after he started consulting Siobhan. The mystery of it all was, why was she practicing in Dublin? She could have been in Manhattan or Harley Street. Why Dublin?

Allan's father had been aware for some time, that Allan needed help, or as he called it, 'psychological intervention.' He had asked a couple of his friends discreetly, who they would recommend. Three names were provided. One practicing in England, one in Vienna and the other at the Tel Aviv University. Instead of them doing an assessment on Allan, he interviewed them. He reasoned it was his mind, his life and he wasn't going to have his mind labeled, by what he termed as a 'bunch of theorists.'

None of them suited him. It was when he was in Dublin nearly a year later, he watched Siobhan being interviewed on a late night special show.

There had been a horrific plane crash near Shannon, leaving only three survivors from the four hundred and seven passengers and crew on board the Boeing 747.

Siobhan was the Trauma Expert. Brought in by American Airlines to advise and set up the Trauma Unit, to assist the relatives of the deceased and various emergency agencies involved. Allan watched the interview.

He had never seen a woman so self-possessed.

She answered the interviewer's questions with empathy, respect and dignity, not only for the bereaved families and the audience of this live show; but also with the knowledge that like 9/11, anyone riveted to their TV screen could also be at risk for vicarious trauma.

This was a woman who was simply unaware of her own beauty; she wasn't advertising herself and was totally unimpressed by her own status as an expert.

Allan researched her background, noting she kept a very low profile. She wasn't married, didn't seem to have a closet full of lovers or burial mounds of ex-lovers. Her published articles proving her theoretical and experiential claims were frequent. It seemed she had a long and committed focus on the subject of adult survivors of child abuse.

He made his own appointment to consult her.

Siobhan didn't make any attempt to assess him. There was no barrier between them. No desk or table, no notebook or pen, just her. He felt he melted into the ambience she had created to work in.

She had booked a double session for him explaining it was more practical for their first meeting, 'however,' she emphasized, 'you are at perfect liberty to use your own discretion. To stop, or leave the session at anytime you feel too uncomfortable to continue.'

He felt empowered. Within fifteen minutes of sitting opposite her, his story started to trickle out and then the flood gates opened.

Siobhan listened to Allan. Her eyes focused on his face. She recognized how his mental agony was being passed through his body. Beads of sweat lingered around his hairline, jaw muscles tightened, hands locked so tightly together the fingers left their imprints above the knuckles. His left knee moved up and down, up and down, faster and faster.

'His body is remembering, God help him.' she thought.

No matter how many disclosures she heard, child abuse never failed to elicit emotions of sadness and anger deep within her. Nothing was ever the same, every victim was unique.

Allan's case was one of the worst sado-incestuous ordeals perpetrated on a child. There was no doubt in her mind, that had it not been interrupted, Allan would not have survived.

Allan was exhausted, physically and emotionally. Dry of all feeling, except numbness around his heart and in the pit of his stomach. Though her face was calm, the compassion which flowed from the woman opposite him was palpable.

'What now?' he asked Siobhan.

'Now you start the longest journey of your life,' she replied.

'When do we start?'

'You've already started.'

His mind returned to the session and his surroundings, Allan explained other difficulties he had, since their last meeting. These were subjective to his feelings and opinions around his work and social life. Just mentioning them to Siobhan seemed to bring him to his own conclusions. There was never any psychological sparring between the two of them; he called his sessions with Siobhan, the Ex-Lax of his mind.

'I've been considering starting a Foundation or a Trust Siobhan, for survivors of CSA (child sexual abuse). The ones who seemed to have slipped through the net of any social services funding. What do you think?'

Siobhan was aware of some of Allan's philanthropic work. The question didn't surprise her. None of his charities and benevolence appeared under his name; all of them were donated and sifted through so many companies the link could never be traced to him.

She also knew Allan was just running the idea past her. He was very well informed that Siobhan insisted never to cross a boundary beyond her own expertise. If a case went beyond her own knowledge she referred her client to the appropriate expert in that field.

She rarely gave her opinions to clients, preferring instead they came to their own conclusions.

'I've been thinking in particular to the survivors of Institutional abuse Siobhan.'

'That sounds an interesting project Allan.'

'Mmm.... I'll have my people investigate it,' he replied.

After Allan left Siobhan opened all the windows. The scent of Lavender wafted into the room once more. Kicking off her shoes she breathed deeply and exhaled slowly, she gradually leaned over; her hair fell like a wave in front of her exposing the nape of her neck and the perfect arch of her back. Without bending her knees, she touched her toes. After a minute she slowly straightened her back then reached her arms high above her head, as if she was trying to pick an invisible apple from an imaginary apple tree.

Sessions were tense, they invaded her body as well as her mind, both had to be released and cleared before she entered the world of her next client.

Chapter 2

SIOBHAN HEARD Gerard before she saw him.

'Dance with meeeee, come out and dance with meeeeee. Be my love for no one else can end this yearning, di dah di dah de dah de daahhhhhh.'

Looking out of the front window, she smiled. Gerard always made her smile. Six foot four and not a pick of fat on him. A comb-over as broad as an alley, flopped up and down as he tap danced his way up the drive. Reaching into the pocket of his jacket he produced a child's skipping rope and skipped the last few yards up the drive.

Breathless he panted, 'Now wasn't that a great cabaret for you first thing in the morning Siobhan. They don't call me Fred Upstairs for nothing?'

'It was Gerard, how are you this morning?'

'Great, just great Siobhan. Sher who wouldn't be great with the sun shining on those of us who are always right?'

'I think you mean "the righteous" Gerard.'

Gerard grinned at her exposing a set of false teeth he swore, were his Granny's.

Gerard never actually sat in a chair; he reversed into it and parked himself. As Siobhan sat opposite him, crossed her legs and smoothed her pencil, slim skirt, one of the many she always wore, as a simple but ultra-chic uniform. With slender, beautifully manicured fingers she lifted the fine chain around her neck, exposing a diamond pendant in the shape of a spiral. Plain on one side and encrusted with diamonds on the other. It was the only piece of jewellery she ever wore.

Gerard admired everything about Siobhan; she was his own, personal angel.

'Well you're in good humor, that's a lovely jacket, very smart Gerard. Do you have an appointment after your session?'

Gerard fingered the lapels of his jacket proudly.

'I got this in the Oxfam shop for a fiver, thought I'd smarten me self-up a bit Siobhan. The only appointment I have is with an iron and an ironing board. I'm going up to old Mrs. Hayes. God love her, she's terrible with the athereritis.'

Gerard had a remarkable vocabulary; he reinvented words to suit himself.

'The cough on her, it's a wonder it doesn't break her back. Every time she coughs she pisses herself. God help us I don't know where to put me feckin eyes, when I see it dribbling on the floor.

'I told her to give up them ould fags. Sher what else has she got except them things? I know me self how hard it is to be addicketed. Didn't it take me a lifetime to give up the booze?'

'Well you look very nice an………'

'Here we go,' Siobhan thought, as she was interrupted by Gerard.

'He's in full throttle today, better to let him have his head and get it all out.'

Gerard's face changed from the happy smiley to the downcast and sullen.

'Well I tell ya Siobhan I nearly gave the ould bitch a smack before I came out! I tell yah Siobhan, if it wasn't that I remembered the breathin, I'd have given her a crack that'd knock her feckin sideways.

'The feckin mouth on that one.

'I'm tellin ya Siobhan, the dirty feckin mind on her is worse than the smell of a bollix with foot and mouth disease.'

Siobhan took a breath to ask him a question but Gerard burst in again.

'She feckin incinerated that that I'd got the jacket cause "I fancied you" and she said I only started to keep me self clean six months ago, coz you must have told me to clean me self-up; and who did I think I was, wearing half a bottle of feckin Old Spice?

'I warned her, she'd be wearing a bottle of feckin HP sauce if she didn't shut her filthy gob. I'm telling ya Siobhan if it wasn't for the breathin I'd lose me senses, she's enough to start me on the bottle again!'

'Gerard, isn't it great you were able to control your anger with your breathing, well done.'

Gerard didn't look as though he had succeeded in anything. Siobhan waited for him to start talking again.

'Ah sher feck it, yer right, I'm delighted at me self really. Ah feck her. To tell you the truth Siobhan; if that had a happened a year ago, I'd have pulled the feckin door off the hinges and smashed it on her feckin big, wooly head!

'I'm telling ya Siobhan thank Christ for the breathin.'

Siobhan new this statement to be true.

A year ago Gerard would indeed have pulled the door off the hinges. No matter how sorry he was, for the domestic violence he had perpetrated on his wife when he was an alcoholic. He was still out of control once she pressed the right button.

He couldn't win. His wife was relentless, and determined to make the rest of Gerard's life as miserable as her own had been. On the few occasions Siobhan had met the woman her attitude confirmed this.

Gerard barged into Siobhan's thoughts.

'Anywayaz, I was too early fer me bus, so I sat at the bus stop and did me breathin. I was just getting into my vicer…visular…. visulamination thing, when some old fart asked me if I was alright.

'I said to him, "would you ever feck off and mind your own feckin business!"

'Jesus!'

'So yer man said, "Well you looked a bit strange with yer eyes closed and big breaths coming out of yer, I thought yez were having a heart attack!"'

'Jesus, feckin heart attack! I told him I was doin me self-hypnotics. "What's that?" he said, and I told him I trained me self to hypnotize me self. When I get stressed out I do it, and I can be anywhere I want to be.

'"Jaysus," he said, "that's a great thing. Ya mean ya can space travel anywhere like?"

'"I can that," I told him.

'"And where do you travel to?" he says.'

'I told him, I travel to a waterfall on a beach in Tahiti, where I have a beautiful wife in a grass-skirt dancing for me and feeding me figs. Yer man must have been a bit deaf.

"PIGS, PIGS, B'Jayzus ... that'll give ya terrible heartburn, I suffer dreadful with that me self," he says.'

'FIGS, FECKIN FIGS. NOT FECKIN PIGS. Sure what would I be eating a feckin pig for?' I said.

'Jesus Siobhan some people are terrible tick.

'And yer man says, "Ah yeah, them are the things they have in a box at Christmas, aren't they, and was she wearing anything else with the grass skirt?"

'She was,' I told him, 'she was wearing half a coconut shell on each of her tits.

'"Jaysus," he says, "I tell you them foreign women know how to dress. No wonder you were havin trouble with yer breathin!"'

Siobhan smiled at Gerard as he doubled over laughing his head off, his teeth slipped slightly, he pushed them back into place with his thumb.

'And what was the rest of your week like Ger...?' Once again Gerard interrupted her.

'Great, great, not a bother. I'm sponsoring a new fellah. God love him. A nice lad, in a terrible state though. His wife and kids had enough and she got him barred from the house. He's sleeping in a tent in his friend's garden. As soon as he moved outta the house, didn't yer woman bring in a boyfriend? Ah well I suppose she's had enough, no woman can live with a bottle and a man shitting in the bed.

'He was in the Rutland Centre and was dry when he left, but sure ya know how it is Siobhan? Yer have to hit rock bottom before yer come back up. I told him a bit of me story, as you do at these meetings and it frightened the shite out of him.'

Siobhan leaned slightly forward and asked Gerard how many meetings he had been to that week? He ignored the question.

'We had a great celebration Siobhan.

'Jackie boy got his leaving results, and didn't he get enough points to get to UCD. Imagine that? The first one in the history of the family to go to a university. I was feckin walking on water after the envelope came through the door.

'Now he has to apply for the grant, because the feckin Credit Union are knockin on the door every five minutes to get something off the loan.'

Siobhan wanted to get the session under control, she put her hand up, Gerard paused and before he could say a word she frowned at him.

'That's great news Gerard, you must all be delighted.

'Talking about money Gerard, did we not agree last week that you would miss at least two AA meetings and start looking for a part time job? What did?'

'Sure amn't I missin one meeting, today when I do Mrs. Hayes ironing Siobhan? And I'm going to start a window cleaning business!'

'I thought the rheumatism in your arms was causing you a lot of pain and you were frightened of heights Gerard! How are you going to climb a ladder let alone wash a window?'

Gerard looked slightly foolish as Siobhan challenged him. He had forgotten he'd told her a couple of weeks ago; he had turned down two part-time jobs because of the pain in his arms.

'Well they are killing me.'

As if to prove it he started rubbing his arms and wincing.

'And I can't climb a ladder, but I can hold one Siobhan. That's why I'm goin to get that lazy fecker Paddy outta the bed every morning. He can go up the ladder and I'll hold the feckin bucket. Now that's what most people call being an ontra-pen-whore.'

He smiled at Siobhan, waiting for the expected praise. Siobhan thought he had the reasoning power of an eight year old. As much as she would have liked to smile, she decided it was time to rain on his parade.

'I don't think that's very practical Gerard. It means you are creating a job for Paddy, which he doesn't want! He's hung-over every morning and you can't drag him out of the bed. How's that going to work? There'll be murder in the house every morning.

'Can you not think of another job? I hear they are looking for a part-timer in the garage up the road, just to clean up the place. You'd like that.'

'Yeah, I love the cleaning and tidying. Strange how I got me obsession with that, isn't it Siobhan? Fekin good job I did, wid yer woman lying around all day with a fag hangin out of her gob. I suppose it's just another addickidtion?

'The trouble is Siobhan if I got that job I'd be giving everyone a slap if they moved anything. You know me, I even have to measure the table when an ashtray is put on it, to make sure it's straight?'

'Okay, but can we see some results on this project next week Gerard. I know you do great work at the geriatric home and they all love you, but it is voluntary. If Jackie is going to university he'll need money to keep up with his peers, he can't work full-time and even part-time will detract from his studies.

'You need to think about a job which will earn you money and keep you busy enough to help you gradually withdraw from your addiction to AA. Three meetings a day, seven days a week gives you no time for anything else.

'You've been in a recovery for more than ten years now Gerard!'

'I know, I know Siobhan, yer right, so you are. Sher I think I'm getting addickited to Old Spice now!'

'Old Spice Gerard...are you drinking the stuff?'

'Ah c'mon now Siobhan, I'm not that much of an eejit.'

'Why do you think you are getting addicted to it Gerard?'

'Well, I keep sniffin me armpits.'

As if to prove his theory he bent over and put his head under his armpit and sniffs!

'Your armpits...why your armpits?' Siobhan hadn't a clue where this conversation is going.

'Well when I put a dab behind my ears and on me wrists I always put a dab under me armpits for luck.'

'Oh, I understand now. Well maybe you could just put a splash on your face and not on the other places, and then you can smell it all the time.'

'Now that's a good idea Siobhan, I didn't think of that. That'll shut the feckin bitch up. She told me I looked like a feckin gorilla the other day, when she saw me head under me arm.'

'Gerard, did you think about what we discussed last week, being part of the group I am?'

Gerard interrupted her again.

'Did you see the papers yesterday Siobhan?'

Siobhan nodded her head. She was very well informed of media disclosures. Every day clients spewed out their anger at rumors and facts surrounding the issues of child abuse. It highlighted that their own problems were not imaginary, the facts and experiences they had buried so deep for half a lifetime were now public property.

'What kinda judges do we have sitting on their arses in them courts? That priest got community service for assaulting those young lads. Sure he was servicing the community when he was doing that. It's a feckin joke.

'I'd ate him alive so I would, it's a feckin disgrace!'

Siobhan moved her fingers to her pendant; the diamonds caught the light. Gerard blinked slightly.

'Did it bring any memories up for you Gerard?' Siobhan said.

Gerard's face changed. When he stopped smiling he looked ten years older. Siobhan pitied him.

'He's forgotten he's a survivor,' she thought, 'he's gone into victim mode.'

'It feckin brought up a big one up Siobhan.' He was quiet for a minute, no doubt, she thought, deciding whether he would continue with this memory or delete it.

'Of me in the cellar! I tell ya Siobhan I don't think about it much these days, but when I do I just want to kill them. I'd feckin tear them ta bits so I would!'

The room was silent. After a while Gerard looked at her, the anger slowly disappeared from his features, his breathing returned to normal. Siobhan was sure he didn't want to continue with this memory, he was waiting for her.

'It's difficult to avoid all the media cover this subject is getting at the moment Gerard, but you've come a long way.'

Gerard smiled.

'Look at yourself Gerard, and think of all the changes you have made? You are living with the family again and most of the time there is peace and harmony in your life. Try to recognize the achievements you have made and the happiness you bring into the lives of others.'

Siobhan smiled at him gently.

'Ah sure look at us we're all doin great, and to think we'll have a university graduate, well that's the icing on the feckin cake, so it is.'

'Did you think anymore about joining the group I'm setting up Gerard?'

'I did think about the group thing Siobhan, and sher I'll try anything. Only one question though.'

Gerard paused. Siobhan recognizes the twinkle in Gerard's eyes and waited for the question.

'Will it be at the same time as me AA meetings?'

Siobhan looks at him with a slight frown.

'Ah sher I was only having you on Siobhan, get away-outta-that. It'll give me something else to do.

Will it be confidential Siobhan, I'd hate me business going all over Dublin!!?'

Gerard laughs until his teeth start shifting again. As he adjusts them Siobhan thought, 'those teeth have a life over their own and they're out of control.'

'Sure I'm only jokin again Siobhan, doesn't the whole of feckin Ireland know all me business, what with the feckin gob of yer woman, and me smashing up the house for 25 years.'

Gerard stood up and shook out his gangly body. He took the skipping rope out of his pocket.

'See yer at the meeting then Siobhan, take care of yerself now. God Bless.'

Siobhan smiled as she watched him skip down the drive. 'If only we could turn the clock back,' she thought.

'Gerard could have achieved so much in his life. What chance did he have? A lifetime's sentence for mitching from school when he was eight, and stealing a bag of sweets?

He's right about those judges, they have a lot to answer for and one day they will be held accountable. Community Service for that so-called paragon of virtue who sexually abused children in his care. It's a bloody laugh. Talk about fitting the punishment to the crime. They might as well hand-over the children to the pedophiles, they are making it easy enough.'

Siobhan stepped out into the garden, breathed deeply and exhaled slowly. Allowing her anger to leave her body in the controlled way she had devised, and passed on to her clients. She slowly leaned forward, her diamond pendant swinging slightly, and clasped her toes. By the time she had picked her invisible apple off the imaginary tree, Siobhan had released every particle of negative emotion in her mind. Her body was cleared of tension and as loose as a ballerina.

Chapter 3

NORMAN CURSED as he pulled into the lane where he usually parked his van.

'Fuckin EEJIT,' he shouted.

The man from Fitzgerald Plumbing was coming out of a house nearby.

'Is that your fuckin van taking up two spaces, ye fuckin eejit?' Norman growled threateningly.

'Ah keep your hair on for God's, sake amn't I going now,' the plumber shouted back at him.

Norman jumped out of the van, 'are ye takin the piss outta me?' He advanced towards the other man. It was too late for the plumber.

'Holy Mother of God,' he said to himself, closing his eyes he waited for the blow to come!

A minute passed, 'I shouldn't' have had that cup of tea yer woman gave me. Please God don't let me piss myself.'

The blow didn't come. He opened his eyes as far as a squint. As his tight lips unfurled, his jaws slackened and his mouth gaped. In front of him, sitting crossed-legged in the middle of the path, with his eyes closed, was the bald headed, brick shit-house of a man who had threatened him.

The man from Fitzgerald Plumbing was rooted to the spot, he didn't know whether to walk around Norman, or stand still. The only thing that broke the silence was the sound of Norman inhaling and exhaling, inhaling and exhaling. It was contagious; the plumber's own breathing involuntarily mimicked the sound.

Norman opened his eyes.

'What the fuck are ye lookin at?"

The plumber was speechless.

'Well are ye goin to move yer fuckin van or what?'

'I am, I am, and I'm sorry for the inconvenience.'

He rushed past Norman, leapt into his van and took off with a screech and smell of burning rubber. Norman parked his van and walked in the direction of Siobhan's office.

Siobhan's first thought on opening the door to Norman was: 'clothes don't make the man, but it's about time he changed his ex-con appearance. I wonder if he actually knows how intimidating he looks.'

Norman's rippling muscles burst through a navy blue, sleeveless vest. Sweat pants clinched at the waist, with a broad leather belt, emphasized its narrow proportions. Black trainers completed the uniform he wore winter or summer.

'How are you Norman?'

'Not so bad Siobhan and yerself?'

'I'm fine thank you Norman.'

'Ye look tired Siobhan.'

Siobhan ignored the remark. It was always the same greeting and the same observation. It was Norman's way of trying to highjack the session by undermining her good health. It was less the concern over her health, more the excessive desire to create anxiety with regard to her looks. It didn't work but he had been repeating it for two years, the repetition was boring. In a fifty minute session there were more important things to consider, she couldn't waste time on trivialities or game-playing.

'How has your week been Norman?'

'Jesus Siobhan, de ye have te always start off the session with the fuckin "Norman" business, ye know I hate that fuckin name?'

'So what do you suggest Norman, and please don't ask me to call you Nut Cracker?'

Norman's nickname had been earned during his stint in a private army in Africa. It seems he gained the title, for cracking the testicles of his foes with a standard issue boot. He claimed he could hear them crack. Siobhan claimed it must have been his imagination as there were no bones in a testicle.

'Well it's better than fuckin English pansy "Norman." Sure no one calls me Norman except you Siobhan.'

'Perhaps I don't feel comfortable with Nut Cracker.'

'Well as you would say Siobhan, that's your problem!'

'You're right Norman, it is my problem. So how about we compromise and I call you, either, Nut or Cracker?'

'Why?'

'Because put the two together and I might as well be calling you 'ball crusher.'

'Well that's why I got the nickname Siobhan!'

'I know Norman. So what will it be? Nut or Cracker?

'You win Siobhan, let's see umm, er, Cracker then. Otherwise ye'll end up calling me fuckin Nuts!'

'Fine by me Cracker, I rather like it, it suits you.'

'So how has your week been?'

'Jacyntha had another one of her breakdowns and went off to hide with her fuckin sister! That bitch won't let me see, or speak to her. She slams the phone down on me every time I ring.'

Siobhan tried to do a quick, mental rewind, attempting to ascertain how long since there had been a similar occurrence. Once she realized the intervals between the events were becoming further apart, she could respond.

'What happened Cracker?'

'Sure the usual thing Siobhan. I went out on Wednesday for a couple of jars after work. Now it was only two beers, I didn't have any shots. Jayzus I got in the door and she laid into me, shouting and screaming that she could smell a woman off me!

'I told her would she ever fock off and where's me fuckin dinner?

'Well one thing led to another and she started to throw my stuff around the place. I warned her Siobhan, but she ignored me.

'Then didn't' she pick up the last fuckin Award I got for me poetry, stamped on it and smashed half the room up. Well I tell ye Siobhan, I fuckin lost me head.'

Cracker leaned forward in the chair, rubbing his sweaty palms along the knees of his sweat pants. He was in no hurry to recount the drama of that evening.

'What happened then Cracker?'

'Sure ye know what it's like Siobhan?'

'What happened Cracker?'

Cracker's voice rose threateningly. Siobhan wasn't frightened or intimidated by Cracker, she knew how volatile he could be and took every reasonable precaution to protect herself during his sessions. Cracker hadn't initially consulted her through the usual channels.

Her clients came to her because they wanted change in their life; they recognized personal change was their own responsibility. Cracker had been ordered by a hard-nosed judge to get himself sorted or else.

His first few sessions with her consisted of cat and mouse childish games. His attempts to manipulate her with lies and flirting were pathetic. Eventually she told him to cut the crap and stop wasting her time and his. He laughed his head off, held his hands up and surrendered.

From that day the work started. It was difficult and excruciatingly painful for him. He had come a long way; however there was still a long journey ahead of him. Old habits die hard when reactions to certain situations and stimuli, were deeply embedded in Cracker's psyche. Underneath the aggressive, angry and sometimes dangerous man, slept a little boy frightened of his own shadow.

'I fuckin warned her enough times. "Don't be fuckin starting on me as soon as I come into the house and don't be fuckin accusing me of going with women."

'And if I do go with other women Siobhan, isn't it her fault. For focks sake, how long am I meant to go without sex?'

'Mmm, mmm?'

She sat quietly accepting his angry glare without flinching.

'Mmm, mmm?' he repeated.

Siobhan remained passive, retaining eye contact with Cracker until he eventually got the message that she was not responding to mumbling, garbled questions.

'Sure half the time it's her fuckin imagination.'

'Was it her imagination this time Cracker? Siobhan asked him, her voice so low it was only just audible. It had taken Siobhan a long time to master what she called 'intonation.'

It was her theory that intonation should be part of the curriculum in every prep school.

It was the natural speech form one of her professors articulated. A man she had great admiration for. His specialty was forensic psychology, and criminal behavior.

Siobhan had spent six months doing post Grad studies and research in the States; she was thrilled and honored when he chose her to be his temporary assistant. That was until her first visit to the infamous Rikers Island Correctional Facility.

A virgin, untapped and ignorant of any experience with criminal behavior, Siobhan still felt the embarrassment of her first day accompanying him. A man of few words with his students, he instructed her to return back to her apartment. Change from her one and only business suit into her oldest street clothes. Remove her makeup, her gold drop ear rings and any jewellery she was wearing. Delete the pony tail and pin her hair tightly to the back of her head.

It wasn't that he preferred she remain unattractive. With Siobhan's natural beauty that would have been impossible. On the drive to Rikers, he explained in the most direct way that working with convicted criminals the risk of violence was extremely high. Drop-ear rings and a pony tail were as tempting for a perpetrator as putting a bleeding body in front of a shark.

Perps scream and shout, it isn't so much a behavioral tactic, it was more about learned behaviour and the fact they had rarely been listened to as children.

The softer her professor spoke, the calmer the perps became. His voice was almost hypnotic. Over the years she had developed her own tone and pace of speech.

Cracker decided to break the silence.

'Now ye know I can't lie to you Siobhan. As ye said in the beginning, there's no point in me sitting in front of ye and lying through me teeth.

'Sure you're the only woman who saw through the bullshit, and I'm glad ye did. At least I'm comfortable enough to be able to tell the truth when I'm here.

'But I'm telling ye Siobhan, if she doesn't get off her arse and give me what I need, I won't be responsible for my actions.'

Siobhan repeated her question.

'Was it her imagination this time Cracker?'

'Well not technically, I suppose.'

'Sure, it was nothing, a quick shag up against the wall in the car park. It's not like we were in bed together.'

Cracker shrugged his shoulders. 'I didn't even know the woman.' His face changed, his voice became louder and more menacing.

'I've been without if for three weeks Siobhan, whadda ye want me to do. Mmmm, Mmm?'

'I say, whadda ye want me to do?'

The louder Cracker shouted the softer Siobhan's voice became. Trading a statement for a reply, she said. 'I have no expectations of you Cracker?'

He sat in silence, his lips moving slightly, he seemed to be unaware he was talking to himself.

'So Cracker, do you feel it's Jacyntha's responsibility because you had shag up against a wall with a complete stranger?'

Cracker's body language became increasingly agitated. Siobhan realized his anger was building and decided to go for broke.

'Was it also Jacyntha's responsibility that you gave her an STD infection five months ago?

'And a few weeks before that, was it Jacyntha's responsibility when you gave her a beating bad enough to put her in the hospital?

'Ye women are all the same, he growled. If she kept her fuckin mouth shut and acted like a real wife, it wouldn't have happened!'

Slowly his anger subsided and he looked at Siobhan; she was surprised to see tears forming in his eyes.

'I'm a fuckin bastard a fuckin eejit so I am!'

'Well that's a start, Siobhan said, 'at least this week you've taken responsibility for your own behavior. Well done Cracker.'

Cracker held his head in his hands, squeezing the temples as if in pain.

'I hate someone shouting and screaming at me. I hate being accused of something. I hate being caught out. A fuckin woman is meant to be quiet and show some respect. Mmm, Mm?'

'What was it you told me about respect and how it was when you were a Mercenary? You mean that respect is earned?'

Without waiting for a reply from her he started to shout again.

'C'mon Siobhan, that's in the fuckin army, not in me own fuckin home!'

Siobhan decides to challenge Cracker's irrational beliefs. 'It's not so much he's a chauvinist,' she thought, 'it's his insistence with bullying everyone around him, especially women.'

'So now you categorize respect. How much do you respect yourself?'

'Whaddya mean?' He looked at her with contempt.

'Respect. Respect yourself Cracker. How much do you respect yourself when you are shagging a strange woman up against a wall, in a public place?'

Cracker frowned.

'Did you think you were using her?'

Cracker hated it when he was challenged, he felt cornered. Siobhan continued before he could even answer the question.

'She was using you and she got what she wanted!'

'Whaddaya mean?'

'Did you think she wanted you?' Cracker didn't reply.

'She wanted a shag. You, a grown man, with your pants down, in a public place, what are you like Cracker?'

'Whaddaya mean?'

'You got your end off and then what?'

'Whaddya mean?' Cracker was starting to think Siobhan was talking in a foreign language. What the hell were all these questions about, he thought?

'Well, what else did you get out of it? Was it a loving experience? Was it a tender experience?'

'No,' he said.

'It was just a shag fer Christ sake!'

Siobhan sat back looking and feeling totally relaxed. She twisted her pendant, the diamonds sparkled. Cracker nervously started to bite his finger nails. He was beginning to feel tired, not just normal tired, exhausted tired.

'So, looking back on it Cracker, how do you feel now?'

'Disgusted.'

'With whom?'

'With me self.'

'What else do you feel?'

'Used.'

'And?'

'Abused.'

'Okay, can you put those two words together and say them five times please.' Cracker's voice became weaker with every repetition, the last one being a whisper.

'Used and abused.'

Siobhan's voice was like melted chocolate to his ears. He became quiet and more relaxed.

'What does that remind you of Cracker?'

Tears are now running down Cracker's face. He moves as if to wipe them with the back of his wrist, and then realized he didn't have a cuff to absorb the moisture. Siobhan leaned forward and slowly removed a few tissues from the box and gently handed them to him.

Sitting down again she could hardly hear his reply.

'What they did to me!'

Siobhan waited for a minute. She felt a deep pity for the man in front of her, but she had to allow him to reach his own awareness of his destructive behavior. The only way to achieve this was by challenging him.

'And now who is doing it to you?

'Me self. I'm doing it, I always fuckin do it'

The diamonds in her pendant caught the light as she moved her position.

'What would you like to do to 'them' Cracker?'

'There's one I'd like to twist the fuckin neck off him, tear his head off!'

He looks down at his feet trying to avoid Siobhan's steady gaze.

'I love her ye know Siobhan?'

'I know you do Cracker. You have self-control; you proved that in the anger-management course. Why do you think you can't use control when it comes to Jacyntha?'

'She fuckin presses me buttons, she fuckin knows how to get to me, she knows exactly how to get to me.'

'And how does she get to you?'

'It's like she uses me, and then throws me away.'

'Can you try to give me one word which describes how you feel when that happens?'

Cracker sat back.

'I fuckin hate it when she gives me this one word business. I could give her a million words and she'd still tell me to give her just one word.'

'Powerless!'

'If you have lost your power Cracker, who do you think has it?'

'She has, she fuckin has it.'

'Yes,' said Siobhan.

'As soon as you start abusing her she has gained what you have lost, even though it might hurt her.

'You have already hurt her emotionally; you make it obvious every time you go with another woman. She's not big enough to hurt you physically, but she can goad you and hurt you emotionally. Who does that remind you of?'

The muscles in Cracker's face tightened, his eyes became slits as he whispered,

'Them bastards.'

Siobhan nodded her head.

'Yes, you were too small to fight back, and as we have discussed before, you feel guilty about that. It has become distorted and you think you were complicit in some way. What was the mantra you developed when you first came into therapy?'

'I was the child, it wasn't my fault.

'I was the child, it wasn't my fault,

'I was the child, it wasn't my fault.'

There was silence between them, a comfortable silence. Cracker felt as if he had come through a war zone

'God, Siobhan, will I ever be normal?' he whispered.

'For most of us Cracker,' she replied, 'normal means being in control in a positive way. That means control of ourselves, not controlling others. All that is, is bullying and a bully is a coward. What happened to your breathing when all that started last week?'

'Jesus, I don't know. What always happens when I have a drink, I suppose. I feel strong and in control. I forget everything.'

'Which is why,' she said, sternly to him, 'you made a verbal contract with me not to drink any alcohol for three months?'

'Yes, and as usual I fuckin broke the agreement.'

'Can we take up the agreement again Cracker?'

'That's okay with me Siobhan, I'll try not to let you down again,' he replied.

'You're not letting me down Cracker. You are letting yourself down, so please try to think carefully before you take another drink.'

'Ah sure maybe I'll avoid the pub altogether.'

'What about your breathing combined with your self-hypnosis, are you having any problems with that?'

Cracker was enthusiastic as he answered that question.

'None, it's the only thing that keeps me sane. It's me escape, the only way I can let go safely and not worry if I am in control.'

He omitted to tell her about the run-in he'd had with the plumber earlier. Siobhan smiled at him.

'Good, well done Cracker.'

Cracker felt something stir within him. 'Christ when she smiles at me like that, she's a cross between the fuckin Virgin Mary and Marilyn Monroe,' he thought to himself.

'Did you think any more about joining the group,' Siobhan asked him? 'You remember I mentioned it to you the last time you were here?'

'I did Siobhan,' he said 'but, shite, ye know I'm a bit of a loner. I've seen half of those fuckin losers at the odd compo meetings. Give me the fuckin creeps they do. Sure most of them haven't had a job in their lives Siobhan. I don't really want to mix with them.'

'That's very judgmental Cracker,' she said. 'Whether you like it or not you've shared similar experiences and every one of you deals with it in your own way. Could it be that you are frightened to look into their eyes in case you see your own reflection?'

'Jesus,' he thought, 'she has an answer for everything.'

'Maybe, I don't know. Well I'll do it for ye Siobhan.'

'No, Cracker you can't do it for me. Do it for you or don't do it at all,' she stated.

'As I explained to you, you are all at a similar stage in your therapy. The only problem I feel, is that you are all isolating yourselves. It's time to bury the shame and feel proud you are survivors, no longer victims. Sharing your experiences of the past and the difficulties of the present are part of moving on.

'I feel you can all do it quicker by doing it as a team. We are not meeting as a social club; this is a very important part of the therapeutic process.'

'If you say so Siobhan.' He was thinking he would tell her what she wanted to hear, and then just not show up.'

'Can you commit to coming to the first meeting? You can leave if you feel uncomfortable. You can even sit right next to the door so you can slip out anytime you want, how would that be Cracker?'

'Ah sure what have I got to lose,' he said?

'Go on then, put me name down. But if there are any fuckin weirdo's I'm outta there!'

'Cracker we need to look at the possibility of you and Jacyntha having Couples Counseling.

'What do you think?'

Cracker looked at Siobhan as if she had gone mad.

'Jesus, Jacyntha'd never do that. She thinks she's the fuckin Virgin Mary and her brothers are the twelve fuckin apostles; and I fuckin know her sister is Mary Magdalene because I focked her on me own wedding day.

'Yer jokin me Siobhan? Jacyntha is all right; as long as she's the victim she's half happy because she can screw me arse to the floor.'

Siobhan thought 'if only it were that simple. Their home is a battle ground and the fall- out affects everyone.'

'It is time both of you thought about and considered the effects, of yours and Jacyntha's behavior, on your son. He's fourteen now and already has an eating disorder. Both of you are using him as a form of emotional blackmail against each other and it has to stop.'

'I know Siobhan, but tell her that she's the one who's feeding him a load of lies behind me back, instead of feeding him a good fuckin steak!'

There was no point in pursuing this problem now, she thought. She needed the two of them to discuss this issue and how to resolve it.

'We'll talk about it next time Cracker. You take care of yourself.'

'I will Siobhan, but you take care of yourself, don't know what any of us would do without you.'

Siobhan went out into the garden, she had half an hour before her next client. Lifting her face to the sun, she closed her eyes.

'He's moved on so much' she thought. 'If only I could get him and Jacyntha into couples counseling, we would be able to get some humane boundaries around their relationship. They are addicted to this unpredictable, unstable and potentially dangerous way of life. He's like a stick of dynamite and she holds the box of matches. They are so codependent neither of them have the courage to step out of the relationship, even for a short time. One day it will explode and the consequences didn't bear thinking about.'

She shivered as an icy chill ran through her body. A vision of a six year old boy cames into her mind. 'What the hell did he do to deserve the torture he went through? Well what the hell did any of them do? Nothing. Poor Cracker, bad enough at six, losing your mother but to be dragged away from your father and two brothers and thrown into an Institution was madness.

'The incompetent, alcoholic Parish Priest who instigated the destruction of Cracker and his family had a lot to answer for.'

Siobhan looked at her watch, she had twenty minutes left. Enough time to have a hot shower, she thought. Sometimes even the sun and gentle exercise couldn't delete the stress of a session. The power shower and minor visualization of standing under a waterfall freed her mind and reinvigorated her.

Chapter 4

THE MAN sitting in the silver Santa Fe was always at least fifteen minutes early for his appointment with Siobhan. He needed the time to compose himself.

Composure for Dezzie was assuming a hangdog expression. He was always sad, always wretched and downcast. It took a certain amount of energy to stabilize his facial expression to portray his feelings of total dejection. Once he had achieved 'the look,' he had the ability to preserve it for the fifty minutes of his session with Siobhan. The only difficulty he had was if she went into what he termed her 'challenge mode.'

He could sometimes make himself impenetrable by becoming silent; it was a bit of an effort to accomplish this state and not always achievable.

This was not a game he played, it was a precaution. He had learned a long time ago that silence did not expose him to risk and injury.

Siobhan watched Dezzie from the window. 'Damn it', she thought. 'That idiot hypnotherapist he once consulted has a lot to answer for; those people should be regulated and monitored more carefully. At least the counseling regulators have made it a lot safer but it still does not prevent anyone putting a brass plate up outside their door.'

It always amazed her at how carefully people invested their money in objects, the research they did, the questions they asked. Yet when it came to investing in their own mental health and well-being, they simply closed their eyes and pointed at a name in the Yellow Pages. The majority of people hadn't a clue about accreditation.

Dezzie had lost one valuable year in his life. He had consulted a hypnotherapist with regard to his addiction to nicotine. The hypnotherapist was so lazy; he used a tape recorder to induce a mind-altering state. Whilst he sat, with his back to Dezzie playing Bridge on his computer! When Dezzie unexpectedly suffered a severe abreaction with a recovered memory, the hypnotherapist panicked and threw him out on the street.

Notwithstanding one bad experience, Dezzie then consulted a counsellor who wasn't accredited and had no expertise in child abuse. The counsellor felt sorry for him, his ridiculous diagnosis for Dezzie was, 'loneliness.'

For six weeks the anti-social Dezzie, who didn't have the ability to use the word, 'NO,' was persecuted into eating a meal at the counsellors' kitchen table. Not only had the counsellor breached confidentiality, because poor Dezzie also had to endure the company of a dysfunctional wife and four noisy children.

Every time the counsellor left the room, his wife bombarded Dezzie, with complaints and full-blown descriptions, of her husband's total lack of prowess and competence in the bedroom department.

Siobhan could not ask Dezzie to write a letter of complaint to the relevant watchdogs. He had extremely low self-esteem. Putting him under that pressure would achieve nothing, except undermine his confidence and sense of self-worth even more.

Siobhan could not tolerate professional ignorance or abuse. Under the guise of client, she made appointments to consult both, the hypnotherapist and the counsellor.

Half way through a session with each, when neither had bothered to even do an assessment, she let them have the full force of her opinion. Her softly spoken, but aggressively intimidating stance had terrified them into submission. Both made a commitment they would seek further training and competency in their field.

The door of the Santa Fe opened. Siobhan sighed as Dezzie heaved his overweight body from behind the steering wheel. Inactivity had rendered him semi-immobile. She watched as the pressure of standing made Dezzie grimace. It had been more than a year since he had ignored the Orthopedic Consultant's advice to have a knee replacement. Dezzie's steadfast refusal to improve his physical health was almost as resolute as his refusal to improve his emotional health.

'Good morning Dezzie' she enquired, 'how are you?'

'Not very good,' he replied.

Siobhan waited until he sat down. It took some effort, to position himself in the chair to become reasonably comfortable. Reaching behind his head, he tightened the elastic band, which secured his ponytail. He did not look well, there were dark circles under his eyes and his skin had a yellow tinge to it.

'He hasn't been out of the house since his last session,' she thought.

'I am sorry to hear that Dezzie. Would you like to tell me about it?'

'Not really,' he replied. He was looking at the floor and obviously did not want to make eye contact with her.

Breaking the silence Siobhan said softly, 'I sense you are very sad today Dezzie. I really appreciate you coming; it is very courageous of you. A lot of people would have cancelled or just not turned up.'

Dezzie did not react; they both sat in silence.

'Have you spent a lot of time this week in the cupboard Dezzie?'

'Yes,' he whispered.

'Dezzie, can you just give me one word which would describe to me how you are feeling right now?'

'Dead.'

'Thank you Dezzie.'

Dezzie sobbed silently, the tears flowed down his face. 'God help him,' Siobhan thought. 'If only he would come out of his self-imposed isolation.'

'The pain will never go away,' he said.

'What pain Dezzie?'

'The pain of being alone.'

Siobhan held onto that thought for a while, she recognized his loss but this was not a session devoted to bereavement.

'How has your health been this week Dezzie?'

'The same,' he said.

'Have you thought any more about taking the Atripla drug Dezzie?'

'No, I don't want to. What for anyway?'

'Okay what about the anti-depressants, why don't you start taking them?'

'No, I don't want to.'

'Dezzie, its difficult enough living with HIV, your depression makes it even worse. Would you not even try the anti-depressants for a couple of months? At the moment it is like you are sitting in a dark room, there's a light beside you but you're refusing to put it on!'

'I DON'T WANT TOOOO SIOBHAN. You say the same thing to me every week!'

Siobhan moved the box of tissues nearer to him; he takes a few and mops his face.

'I saw Nigel again last night.'

'Do you want to tell me about it Dezzie?'

Shrugging his shoulders as if there is a great weight upon them, he sighed and finally made eye- contact with Siobhan.

'He was sitting on the end of my bed, smiling at me.'

'Did he say anything to you?' Siobhan asked him.

'The usual, like a voice in my head. He told me he loved me and he was waiting for me.'

Siobhan had little belief in apparitions or ghosts; however, Dezzie had a complete lack of anything tangible to hold onto in his life. There was no point in challenging his belief that every now and then his deceased lover paid a nocturnal visit.

'How long did he spend with you this time?'

'I don't know. I lose track of time when he visits me.'

Siobhan how much longer is it going to take me to die?

'I don't know Dezzie.'

Dezzie was silent for a while. 'I seem to have been waiting a lifetime.'

'We all wait a lifetime Dezzie. We are born, we live, and we die. In the meantime, it's all about how we live, and the choices we make.'

'I made my choice when Nigel died,' he said.

Siobhan decided it was time to move the session on and gently tried to stimulate justification of his statement.

'Perhaps you made your choice before that Dezzie?'

Dezzie, forgot to use his silent routine. His automatic reaction to Siobhan's statement was a question.

'What do you mean?'

'When Nigel was diagnosed with HIV,' Siobhan replied, 'your choice was to have unprotected sex with him. Wasn't it?'

'Yes. I thought we would die together. I wanted to die with him. He was my life.'

'That must have been a very difficult decision Dezzie?' she said.

'No. It was easy. I knew when he was dying that all I was going to have was that empty space again. How was I to know that HIV could go on indefinitely without getting full-blown AIDS. Waiting for it is agony.'

'I am sure it is Dezzi. Why don't you stop waiting and start living your life?'

'I DON'T WANT TO.'

Dezzie became agitated. 'HOW MANY TIMES DO I HAVE TO TELL YOU, AND EVERYONE ELSE? I JUST WANT TO BE LEFT ALONE IN MY EMPTY SPACE!'

There was silence; neither of them felt the need to break it.

'I feel tired Siobhan The kind of tiredness that gets into your bones. It gets into everything except my head. My head is spinning with thoughts, one after the other, one after the other, so quick I can't seem to make sense of them.'

'Would you like to try your relaxation, and thought stopping technique, with me Dezzie?'

'Okay,' Dezzie replied not really bothered one way or the other. 'Might as well I suppose.' He leaned his head back in the chair and stared at the ceiling.

Siobhan slipped the pendant out of her shirt, and spoke to Dezzie quietly. Gradually his breathing became calm, his eyes closed and his body relaxed. He became responsive and aware when Siobhan asked him if he had returned to his empty space.

'No, I'm here with you and I feel safe. I wish I could feel like this all the time Siobhan.'

'Do you remember when the empty space started Dezzie?' She sat back in her chair waiting for Dezzie to get his thoughts in order.

'It started when she locked me in the cupboard.'

'Do you mean, when you were a little boy with your foster mother?'

'Yes. She wouldn't let me talk. She wouldn't let me sleep in my room unless when he was there. I could melt into that cupboard. It was my empty space. I think I was lucky to have an empty space.'

'Why, Dezzie?'

'You know why Siobhan I've told you so many times.'

'Yes and sometimes talking helps stop the pain. Do you remember how old you were Dezzie?'

'Four, just four years old. When I went into the empty space in the cupboard, I didn't feel the pain.'

'What pain Dezzie?'

'Of the knotted rope and wire coat hanger! I don't want to talk about it anymore Siobhan. I feel comfortable right now and I don't want to lose this feeling.'

'That's okay Dezzie.'

Dezzie started to weep like a child; Siobhan's heart went out to him, as it would to any child. She did not attempt to stop him, knowing the sorrow would subside when the emotion diminished.

'When I do my breathing Siobhan, I go back into the cupboard, into my empty space.

'What's it like in there Dezzie?'

'It's warm, I can float. It's comfortable and safe.'

'Do you feel angry when you are in there, or do you feel sad?'

'I can feel anything I want to feel. I can be anyone I want to be,' he said.

Dezzie started to dissociate. His voice changed to that of a three year old.

'Sometimes I'm a happy boy.'

Then his voice changed to a ten year old. 'Sometimes I am a warrior with a big sharp sword and

I can kill people....cut them up into little pieces. And sometimes.'

Siobhan encouraged him to continue. 'Sometimes Dezzie?'

'Sometimes. Sometimes, there's a lot of blood, but it doesn't hurt, it doesn't hurt and I'm not frightened.'

'Whose blood is it Dezzie?"

Dezzie's voice was strong and in control. 'Sometimes, HIS.'

'And sometimes?' Siobhan prods him gently, her voice so low it is almost a whisper.

Dezzie's voice returned to the child once more.

'Mine. It's mine and I have to clean it up. CLEAN IT UP YOU BASTARD, CLEAN IT UP!'

'Who is telling you to clean it up Dezzie?

'She is. CLEAN IT UP YOU BASTARD, CLEAN IT UP YOU BASTARD, CLEAN'

He stopped suddenly. His eyes shifted quickly from side to side, as if he was not quite sure where he was. He looked at Siobhan.

'It's okay Dezzie, you're safe, you are safe.' Siobhan allowed him time to collect his thoughts and become aware of his surroundings.

Dezzie looked more responsive than when he came into his session. His hangdog expression has disappeared; instead of silent resignation, he looked more alert.

'Do you still feel sad Dezzie?

'No'

'What do you feel now?'

'Angry.'

'Who are you angry with?'

'GOD.'

'Why God?'

'Cause he took every normal thing away from me when I was born, and gave me nothing in return. When I was born I deserved all the love and nurturing every baby gets. AND WHAT DID I GET? SOD ALL.'

'Then when I had someone who loved me, he even took him away from me. I don't think I even believe in God anyway!'

Siobhan felt the session was taking off. He was losing his apathy. Dezzie could only display three emotions, indolence, anger and apathy. She was always slightly relieved when the anger started to come; at least it showed he was emotionally aroused.

'Maybe,' Dezzie continued, 'God is a lunatic who imagined he made the world in six days and rested on the seventh. Maybe he was suffering from the DT's when he said he took a rib out of Adam and made it into a woman.

'Maybe Jesus was on Ecstasy and thought he walked on water.

'Maybe he was already drunk when he said he turned the water into wine. Maybe the cripple was a hypochondriac and not a cripple at all!'

Dezzie stood up suddenly and threw his hands in the air. Siobhan was startled but only raised an eyebrow.

Dezzie shouted, 'MAYBE, MAYBE, MAY BE. I'M, SICK OF MAYBE'S!'

He sat down once more, put his head in his hands and murmured.

'I just want to die Siobhan, I just want to die.'

'It's not your time yet Dezzie,' Siobhan said. 'There is a time to live and a time to die. Everything in this life is about time.

'WHY? WHY? WHY?'

He shouted at her.

'I don't have all the answers Dezzie.'

'No but you have all the questions don't you.

'What the hell is the reason we HAVE to live, when all we want is to die?'

'Okay Dezzie. If you had to give a reason for living, what would it be?'

'I can't think of one reason Siobhan.'

'If you could think of a reason for dying, what would it be?'

'I'm HIV positive Siobhan; I'm going to die anyway.'

'There are always unforeseen possibilities in our life Dezzie, such as being hit by a car. You might not die of AIDS, you have been HIV positive for 6 years and you are symptom free. Your immune system is stronger than mine. I have never even known you to have a cold. Being HIV positive is not valid reason to want to die. Give me another reason why you want to die?' she said.

'I just want to die; I want to be with Nigel.'

Siobhan looked at Dezzie and waited.

'Is that not a good enough reason?' he asked her.

'The ultimate power we have as human beings is the power to choose whether we live, or whether we die. You have never threatened or attempted suicide Dezzie. You don't believe in suicide. You can't wish yourself to death. However you can start to live your life again.'

Dezzie started to weep.

'How can I live my life without Nigel, Siobhan?'

Siobhan leaned slightly towards Dezzie. The tone of her voice was almost hypnotic.

'Nigel lived a life without you. Nigel made his own choices. Get real Dezzie. Stop trying to idealize Nigel. He was a smooth operator; all he did was play different roles! He used you.

'He took your love, your adoration and manipulated it. He picked up rent boys, brought them back to your home and screwed them in front of you. He knew the risk he was taking and he didn't even bother to protect himself. When things went wrong for Nigel, he beat the shit out of you. He made you cry. He was rich and famous and kept you as the slave you were for him. He paid you a salary and when you didn't do what he wanted, he gave you nothing. How many grand houses did he have, and yet he left you with nothing?

'He knew if anything happened to him, you would be on the street. You might have been dependant on him when he was alive, but you can't be dependent on a dead man.'

'I know. I know you are right Siobhan, but what can I do?'

'It's not about being right Dezzie. It's about you spending two years in therapy and still insisting you don't want to get up off your arse and change your life. A lot of this is about secondary gain.'

'What do you mean? I don't understand what you mean?'

Siobhan knew she was coming on strong, but felt she had to activate and arouse his emotions enough, to encourage him to question his own distorted beliefs. She mimicked him.

'I want to die, I want to die, I want to die. It gets you a lot of attention doesn't it?'

Dezzie looked at her in disbelief, he felt slightly embarrassed. It was like looking in a mirror at his own reflection. He wasn't quite sure how to respond.

'I suppose so,' he said.

'Get up and go out with a few friends. Alternatively, why don't you come to the HIV and AIDS Support Group here every Monday night? You'll meet people whom you might have something in common with, and get some support. They all go for a burger or something to eat after the meeting. Why don't you just try it Dezzie?'

'I don't like meeting new people.'

'Dezzie, what do you suggest then. What do you think you could do to make your life a little happier?'

'I don't know?' he replied.

Siobhan did not respond, she had done enough prodding and challenging. Her silence was calm and non-invasive.

Dezzie shifted uncomfortably in his chair, he felt resentful.

'Why,' he thought, 'is she pushing me so hard today?'

'My mother wants to go to Bingo on Thursday night, but she doesn't want to go on her own. She says she can't keep up with the numbers quick enough and keeps nagging me to go with her.'

'Well that would be nice,' Siobhan smiled, 'she does enough for you; it would make a change to do something together.'

'Suppose so.'

'Right. So that's your homework for this week. See how the other half live. Have a few laughs, come back next week, and tell me all about it. You never know between the two of you, you might win a fortune.'

Dezzie resumed his sad face wishing he had never mentioned the Bingo.

'By the way Dezzie, the Gay Helpline is looking for telephone volunteers; maybe you could give them a couple of hours a week?'

Dezzie looked horrified at the suggestion, first Bingo, then Gay Helpline.

'Has she gone off her head?' he thought.

'There are a lot of people out there suffering Dezzie; sometimes we have to give a little to get something back, even if it's only a bloody ear ache.'

Dezzie actually smiled. 'Okay Siobhan. I'll think about it.'

Returning his smile Siobhan asked him how he felt?

'I always feel better when I speak to you Siobhan, I'm okay. By the way I'll come to that group meeting you were talking about last week.'

Siobhan was taken aback with his declaration. 'Wow' she thought, 'perhaps he is ready to come out of his isolation.'

'Good, and don't forget your breathing and self-hypnosis. Sit in a chair and do it Dezzie and try to avoid going into that empty space please.'

'Okay Siobhan, thanks.'

'You're welcome Dezzie,' she smiled fondly at him.

Siobhan stood by the door watching Dezzie. He had to exert a huge physical, effort to squeeze his body behind the steering wheel of his car.

'He holds onto his excess weight, as firmly as he holds onto his distorted beliefs with regard to his relationship with Nigel,' she thought. 'There hasn't been one person in his life that hasn't let him down. Jesus I hate challenging him like that. However, if he only reacts to antagonism so be it. No wonder with the life he has had. Born to a junkie, fostered out to a sadistic, mad psychopath. Then thrown into Letterfrack at the age of six. God love him.'

She waved at him as he reversed out of the drive. He smiled and waved back.

Siobhan was a firm believer in the expression 'you are what you eat'. She had got into the habit of preparing fresh soup every other night, it lasted two days. Chopping vegetables and pounding garlic was therapeutic for her. Taking an hour's break she took the soup into the garden and sipped it slowly. 'Soup, fruit and sunshine,' she thought, 'what else could a girl want?'

Chapter 5

A NEATLY trimmed goatee beard, distinguished the man walking around Siobhan's garden. He could have been anyone's favorite uncle. There was gentleness about his movements, which seemed to embrace the atmosphere.

Siobhan watched as he tenderly placed the plant in a corner, at the rear of the garden.

'This is where he wants to be Siobhan, what do you think? '

'I think it is perfect Ant, thank you so much for your thoughtfulness. Would you like to do the honours?'

'I would love to,' he replied.

Siobhan handed him a trowel. He lightly removed a small mound of earth, took the plant from its temporary home and lovingly positioned it into its natural habitat.

'You water it Siobhan, then he'll know you are his earth mother.'

'Okay, but you talk to it Ant.'

As she slowly poured the water over the plant, Ant quietly spoke.

'Wild Cherry, Prunas Seretona, nurture this space

and bring about reconciliation and inner tranquility, to all who touch you.'

Siobhan was not accustomed to accepting gifts from her clients, this was an exception. Ant had explained to her it was a healing tree and as such, it would improve the health and well-being of everyone who used the garden.

Returning to the room, Ant waited until Siobhan was seated before he took his place.

'You look tired Ant, have you been on nights?

'Yes, just two more to go then I have a couple of days off.'

Ant stroked his beard, he looked thoughtful and sad. Siobhan waited patiently, she knew something was wrong but Ant never needed to be coerced; he would speak when he felt the need to speak.

There was no such thing as a perfect client, some were easier than others. They fought hard to reclaim their lives, by using the various tools she taught them. It was not easy to change deeply embedded reactions to situations and certain stimuli.

Change was a journey into the unknown, it was terrifying or exciting to some. Shattering, distressing and heart-rending to others. It took a huge amount of courage. Once the process started there was no going back. Previous inaccessible memories surfaced one after the other; some so remote they were hardly believable or credible.

Siobhan knew the process very well. She had done the journey and walked the green line. The route towards regurgitating her own biographical pain had overflowed with fear; she had experienced every emotion possible. The person who made-up the expression 'there is always light at the end of the tunnel' failed to reveal there was an inexhaustible amount of tunnels.

There was a slight tremor in Ant's voice.

'We lost Mrs. Ryan last night.' He sat quietly, not requiring or needing any response from Siobhan.

'I am so sorry to hear that Ant, you were very close to her weren't you?'

'I was Siobhan, she was a great character, and lovely women, God rest her soul. Her family is devastated. Six of her kids and eleven of her grandchildren were with her at the end. I suppose you could say, she was surrounded by love, you could actually feel it in the room Siobhan.

'You know Siobhan; just before she died, she opened her eyes, I swear, she looked around her and knew every one of them. Then she said, "where is my Ant?" It was as if the Alzheimer's had gone.

'God I loved that woman, I used to pretend she was my own mother.'

Ant leaned forward in his chair, rested his elbows on his knees, put his head in his hands and cried.

'I'll miss her so much Siobhan.'

Siobhan sat in silence, she too felt sad. Mrs. Ryan had been in Ants' life for a few years. A woman who created life in others she drifted in and out of lucidity. Alzheimer's had its own dark places to visit, places where memories and recognitions were warped. Time-frames were jigsaw puzzles with the corners missing. Clarity for Mrs. Ryan were the years between 1939 to 1960. Her husband went missing in action, though it had never been proven, Mrs. Ryan knew his final resting place had been Dunkirk.

'The eejit left me to fight someone else's war, so he did. Sher all he ever wanted was a bit of peace and quiet, away from the children. Well didn't he get that, so he did? There's no place quieter than a grave, God rest his soul, the eejit.'

By proxy, Ant always brought Mrs. Ryan into his sessions, recounting something amusing, bizarre or loving.

'It's okay Ant, let it out, take your time, you are in a safe place.'

'I'm sorry Siobhan.'

Slowly the tears subsided and Ant's breathing became calm and steady.

'I think you spent more years with Mrs. Ryan then your own mother, didn't you Ant?'

'I suppose I did Siobhan, that's why I feel the loss so much.'

'What age were you Ant when you were sent to live with your grandfather, was it seven?'

Ant unconsciously stroked his beard.

'It was Siobhan. May the devil look after his own bastards? I will never be able to forgive her Siobhan. When I think of Mrs. Ryan rearing six of them, and that ole bitch thinking four was three to many. As long as I live I'll never be able to forgive her.'

'How long is it, since she passed away Ant?'

Ant's sadness was replaced with anger.

'It's been four years Siobhan. I have never shed a tear for her. I still remember the night I went and urinated on her grave.'

Siobhan also remembered that night. She had been woken by the Nokia-tone she had activated on her crisis mobile. The number was only given to clients who were at risk or had suicidal idealization. Night time for some, was a dark, lonely hole. Sometimes it was too deep for them to climb out of. When she answered the phone, it was Ant speaking from a graveyard in County Offaly. He had driven over a hundred kilometers in the middle of the night, obsessed with the desire to urinate on his mother's grave. Ant could not wait until the morning to telephone Siobhan. He felt his achievement warranted a trumpet fanfare. Unfortunately, he did not receive the accolade he had hoped. Siobhan had simply said, 'interesting, we'll talk about it in your next session. Goodnight Ant.'

Her crisis-line was rarely abused, clients knew she worked long hours, every client who was given the privilege of having the number were well-versed in what constituted a crisis.

'What I will never be able to fathom out,' Ant said, 'is, after she went through the abuse herself with that evil bastard. Why did she send me to live with him? Talk about leading the lamb to the slaughter. Why did she do it Siobhan?'

'I don't know Ant,' Siobhan said.

'There is rarely an answer to the word why, and never an answer from a dead person. People did not talk about child abuse in those days. People living in rural areas were very isolated and the common theme with child rearing was "spare the rod, ruin the child."'

'I know,' he replied, 'but surely her own mother, my granny, must have known what was going on?'

'Perhaps she did Ant,' Siobhan replied. 'But who was your grandmother going to tell? Where could she run to with five children?

'In those days there were no shelters for battered women. Who would believe them if they had the courage to tell anyone what was going on? People just did not talk about it. Then there was the shame as well as the fear.

'Didn't your mother tell you, your grandfather kept the shotgun in the kitchen?'

'She did,' Ant replied. 'She told me he shot the puppies in front of all them, because my granny tried to stop him beating my uncle with the leg of a chair.'

'You know that women didn't have a voice in holy Ireland in those days Ant? Sometimes you just have to look at the whole picture.'

Ant stroked his beard for a moment.

'Not just the women Siobhan, what about the children? Look at what happened to me when I opened my mouth? When I think about old Mrs. Ryan, I'm sure she would have done more than open her mouth if her father had done those things!'

'She was one gutsy lady Ant; she probably would have taken the gun and blasted him into the middle of next week. We are not all the same and we have to accept and recognize that.'

Ant started to weep again. 'I'm sorry Siobhan; it's probably because I'm tired.'

'It's okay Ant. You were taking care of Mrs. Ryan for many years. Be kind to yourself. Recognize your loss and allow yourself to grieve. Honour your feelings Ant; they are part of who you are.'

'You know Siobhan, I don't know what I would do if anything happened to you. My life has changed so much since I started coming here.'

He sat silently stroking his beard. Siobhan was well aware Ant had no dependency on her; bereavement brought its own emotions of insecurity, his feelings towards everyone in his life would temporarily become suspect for a little while.

'You've worked hard Ant to get to this stage; it's been a long and very painful journey. Own your courage and persistent determination to change your life. I did not do the work. You did.'

'But,' Ant said, 'I couldn't have done it without you Siobhan.'

'I'm just the interrupter, the person who came into your life and showed you how to use the tools you already had. You made all the changes because you had the resolve to let go of the anger.'

'Yes,' Ant replied. 'I let go of the anger, so why the hell can't I let go of the hatred I still feel for my mother?'

'Perhaps you feel she's responsible for starting a chain of events which escalated out of control,' Siobhan suggested.

'Well, she certainly did that Siobhan. What I cannot understand is…. how can someone who has suffered abuse go on to inflict it on their own children? She knew what that old man was like. I just do not believe that because you have been abused you do the same to your own flesh and blood. If she hadn't sent me to that old bastard, then he wouldn't have shipped me off to the Christian Brothers and none of the rest would have happened, would it?'

Siobhan knew there was nothing she could say to make an unacceptable situation become acceptable. Ant's grief with his recent loss of Mrs. Ryan was overpowering, it was arousing all the other losses in his life and they were fusing together. His job as a nurse in the old people's home made death and dying a daily occurrence. It was the norm within the environment he inhabited. Unfortunately, the transference of his affection to Mrs. Ryan and her fondness towards Ant, changed the relationship from patient to maternal parent. This had been a slow process, it had taken a long time.

Somewhere along the line, Siobhan had missed it.

'As I said Ant. Nothing starts in isolation; there is always one event which has the possibility of starting a chain.'

'Yes,' he replied. 'However, if she hadn't sent me to live with him. There would have been no chain. You cannot have a chain without the first link. She knew he was a pervert. She knew what would happen to me. She was the one. I was the child. It was her fault,' he said.

'Your mother didn't have a voice Ant. In those days, any parent could have their child committed to an asylum, once inside one of those places she would have been forgotten; as if she never existed'

'Siobhan gently moved her diamond pendant. 'Shall we take five minutes out to relax Ant; it will lower your stress levels a bit?'

'Good idea Siobhan, I feel as though I could eat a bucket full of valium.'

Ant leaned back in his chair and breathed deeply.

'Exhale out as if you are blowing through a straw, let out the pain Ant,' Siobhan told him. Gradually she felt the release of her owns stress. When he seemed more relaxed and refreshed, Siobhan attempted to clarify what had been said with regard to being voiceless.

'You remember the beating you endured, when you told the Priest in confession, what was happening to you Ant?'

'Jesus, I'll never forget that beating!' Ant stroked his beard and looked at his right wrist. It was slightly bent. A constant reminder of what had been done to him.

'Didn't they break my wrist, the animals? They hammered me all around the gymnasium; I remember their sweat splashing on me like it was raining. I'm not a violent man, as you know Siobhan, but give me ten minutes alone in a room with that devil and there's only one of us who'd walk out.'

Siobhan nodded her head.

'Apart from the physical and emotional stress of that event Ant, how did it affect your trust in people?' Siobhan asked him. Ant thought for a while, still inspecting his misshapen wrist.

'I never spoke again about what happened to me, not until the day I walked in here,' he said.

'So,' said Siobhan, 'would you say you were rendered voiceless?'

Ant looked at her, shook his head and stroked his beard.

'Now I understand what you mean Siobhan. That beating was a direct result of me telling the priest in confession, what they were doing to me. I suppose you could say that was the first link. The second link being the priest breaking the confidentiality of confession, by telling them what I had said, even though he was probably trying to save me. So the chain was started.'

Siobhan thought Ant was now starting to understand the word voiceless. The short break had allowed his anger to calm.

'Where there is anger,' she thought, 'reason and logic disappear.'

'Yes Ant, 'she said quietly. 'I am not asking you to forgive your mother. I am asking you to look at the bigger picture of chance and circumstance. The anger you feel towards your mother has not dissipated since she died. The anger is being fed by your hatred. The woman is dead. Nothing can touch her. You cannot run away from that emotion, it is consistently breeding resentment, fuelling the fire and preventing you from moving on in your healing. It is like a cancer Ant and the chain keeps growing.'

Ant listened to Siobhan's voice. Totally without accusation or recrimination, she had tried to open his mind and heart to the possibility of change.

'So how do I stop it Siobhan, how do I let it go?' he asked her.

'I suppose by breaking the chain,' she said. 'Maybe you could think about ways of doing that Ant?'

Siobhan could have suggested various techniques to help eliminate this problem. However, she preferred her clients to develop and use their own methods. Siobhan knew Ant was more than capable of doing this. She had the belief that deep inside everyone, was the power to heal mental anguish. Self-research led to self-achievement, which led to the ability to maintain the equilibrium of mind and body. Humanizing oneself was essential for adults who had been dehumanized as children.

Ant was thinking of his own children.

'Jesus, I never laid a hand on any of my three, neither did Sheila. In fact, come to think of it, we were too soft, we loved them too much.'

'You can never love a child too much Ant, never,' Siobhan almost whispered the words to him.

'Yes you are right Siobhan.

'Sheila came with me to do the walk by the Radisson the other day Siobhan. Jesus I can't understand why I still get a panic attack if I have to walk past those gates!'

'It is anxiety attacks now Ant, not full-blown panic attacks. At least you don't have to cross over the other side of the road anymore. The anxiety is from the association. Even though it is a hotel now, the building from the outside looks the same as it did when you were living there. But you are doing well Ant, very well.'

'It sounds crazy to be so terrified of a few bricks and mortar; thank God Sheila is so patient with me.'

'It's not the bricks and mortar Ant, they are just the triggers. It is how your brain has become conditioned to deal with the memories, which terrify you. Many insane things happened in that building when the Christian Brothers had it,' Siobhan said.

Little did Ant know the building gave her the creeps. Before it had been bought and converted into the hotel, Siobhan, under the pretext of being interested in purchasing the property, had gone to view it.

The building was empty. After the initial viewing she asked the estate agent if she could walk through it alone, he waited for her in the main hall.

Siobhan's interest was, for the most part, in the basement area.

Even though the day was warm and humid, there was an icy chill in the corridors and rooms below ground level.

It was sinister and gloomy. Siobhan could almost feel the pain of human oppression and subjugation. It was typical of every little boy's worst nightmare.

Returning to the ground floor, she ran straight out of the French doors and gulped in the fresh warm air.

'I could kill each and every one of them Siobhan, tear them to pieces with my own hands,' Ant said.

'Will I ever get to the stage of being able to go in there and fight my demons Siobhan?'

'I think you will Ant.'

'Siobhan I was wondering if I would be intruding if I went to Mrs. Ryan's funeral. What do you think?'

Siobhan was not expecting this question; she felt she had to normalize her answer.

'I don't think you'd be intruding Ant, the family think a great deal of you; in fact you are almost like one of their own. However, do you think you feel capable of attending?'

Ant stroked his beard and looked thoughtful as if he was weighing up the pros and cons.

'Well,' he said, 'when they put Old Jimmy Flynn in his coffin, and the other week, poor old Breda, I didn't hyperventilate at all.

I haven't had any flashbacks for a good six months. In fact I even touched Breda's coffin. I know I'm still claustrophobic but I'm not associating it with being locked in the coffin anymore. I think I would be able to cope and I would really like to go Siobhan.'

'When was the last time you felt claustrophobic Ant?'

'A few weeks ago when I was in Clery's with Sheila.'

'Now, I would not have gone in the lift if she hadn't have been with me, but we waited 'till it was empty and I didn't have a problem.'

Siobhan smiled at him.

'Well done Ant, that's terrific.'

Ant looked a little bashful, stroked his beard and smiled back at her.

'Do you remember when Sheila and I went to New York, Siobhan?'

'I do Ant.'

'Do you remember the Empire State Building saga Siobhan?' The therapist started to laugh, Ant joined in.

'I do Ant,' she replied.

The moments of sharing an intimate joke or memory, between herself and any client were rare and she savored them.

'Jesus. Sheila and I often laugh about me and the sandwiches walking up the one thousand eight hundred and sixty steps to the top of the Empire State Building. Sheila was like a Sherper coming out of the lift on every floor and waiting for me with the bottle of water.'

Ant stroked his beard and doubled up laughing, Siobhan joined in.

'It took us nearly two hours to get to the top, and then we couldn't see anything because of the fog! In addition, Sheila was so terrified of the height she couldn't even look out at the view. We just sat there and ate our cheese and pickle sandwiches. Then it took us an hour to get down to the street again.

'Imagine one hundred and two floors, and there I am having a problem going up to the first floor in Clery's!'

Siobhan giggled and Ant continued laughing.

'Well,' said Siobhan, 'if you ever want to climb Mount Everest Ant, you've already had a practice run with the Empire State Building.'

'You are right there Siobhan. Anyone who asked us where we had been for our holidays, we told them we took an adventure holiday up the Empire State Building.'

They both laughed again, enjoying the release of all the tension, sadness and anger that had been in the room.

'I was thinking about the group thing you mentioned last week. I think I would like to join it. You don't think the other men attending will want to tear me to pieces do you Siobhan?'

'Why do you ask that Ant?'

'Because of me being an ex-Christian Brother.'

'You're a survivor like the others Ant. It will give them the opportunity to understand the other side of the story. Sometimes I wonder if everyone was a victim in an unstoppable cycle, which just went round and round and round.'

'There were a few good ones though Siobhan, weren't there?'

'Yes Ant, there was. Unfortunately they just didn't have a loud enough voice; they were suppressed by fear as much as the victims.'

'How do you feel now Ant?'

'I feel much better Siobhan, maybe I'll go home and do my breathing and self-hypnosis, then get a good sleep.'

'That sounds good Ant, but don't use your hypnosis to block out your grief, honor your feelings and let them come through.'

'Thanks Siobhan.'

'You are more than welcome Ant, thank you for the beautiful tree I am sure everyone will enjoy it. You take good care of yourself and my best wishes to Sheila.'

'I will, mind yourself now Siobhan.'

Siobhan went into the garden and inspected the small tree of reconciliation and tranquility. She bent over and touched her toes slowly; as she stretched her arms up high the sun filtered around her body making her skirt and blouse almost transparent. She smiled as she visualized herself picking cherries from the tree, once it became full grown.

Chapter 6

BINS DID not have a car. He would love to have had a Mini Minor, simply because it was small like him. Bins told everyone, who would listen, there were too many cars on the roads. He also tried to convince all and sundry they could catch road-rage from driving a car.

The real reason Bins didn't have a car is because; he did not know how to drive.

He had a few lessons but couldn't understand why he had to change gears. He had a few more lessons in an automatic car and couldn't understand why he had to use only one leg. It was all too complicated for him and the traffic lights annoyed him.

He decided he was much better off on his old bike. All he had to do was pedal, squeeze the brakes and jump onto the path to avoid the traffic lights. There was no illegal parking and no way could the bastards clamp his back wheel.

Bins also didn't have a watch; he had never been able to master the fact that there was an a.m and p.m. He did not need a watch; he had the ability to know within a minute or two, the exact time. He used his head as an alarm clock. If he had to wake up at six a.m, he would knock his head on the pillow six times before he went to sleep.

As he leaned his bike against a bush in Siobhan's driveway, he looked behind him, bent over removed the bicycle clips from his ankles, and pushed them above the elbow of each arm.

Watching him from the window, Siobhan recognized his routine and smiled, Bins did not have Obsessive Compulsive Disorder; he had habits, which he rigidly adhered to.

'Good afternoon Bins, how are you today?'

'Grand Siobhan, how's yourself?'

Bins spoke through his nose. Nasal congestion ruled his life but surgery was out of the question. He trusted no one. There was no way he would allow himself to be anaesthetized. He sat in the chair, which faced the door. Bins could not sit anywhere without facing a door, he had to know his quickest route of escape.

'I'm fine, thank you Bins. What was your week like?'

'Ah, de same ould thing Siobhan.'

'How have you been sleeping Bins?"

'De same ould way Siobhan. Under de bed with her on top of me.'

'You mean, you, under the bed, and Maggie in the bed?'

'Yeah, as I said, under de bed and her on top of me.'

'Did you try to sleep in the bed this week Bins?'

'A'h sure, there's no point Siobhan, amn't I all right where I am? Yer woman u'd have a shaggin heart attack if I got in next ter her?' He looked behind him, something he did constantly; it made him feel more secure and relaxed.

'Are you all right Bins?' Siobhan enquired.

'I'm great Siobhan, you know me, as long as I'm facing de door and there's no one sneaking up behind me I'm fine.'

Siobhan sat quietly, patiently waiting for Bins to talk. Over time, she had stopped instigating his sessions with questions. His concentration was poor, he disliked being challenged and she was well aware, that when he had something to say, he would say it. If she was silent, it gave Bins time to get his thoughts in order.

'Martin's back in de Joy!' Bins said.

Siobhan was not surprised at his statement. The majority of the adolescents from Bins estate had experienced incarceration of one form or another by the time they were fifteen. Mountjoy was a Post Graduate course for them, a badge of honour. A place with a bed, three free meals a day and a crash course on how to become a professional criminal.

'I am sorry to hear that Bins.'

'I'm not,' he said. 'I dobbed him in me self, de shaggin fecker!'

'Do you want to talk about it Bins?'

Bins looked quickly behind him.

'I warned him Siobhan. I beat de shite outta him, but would he listen?'

'I telephoned Garda Moriarty and told him to pick him up. On de skag he is Siobhan. Chasing de shaggin dragon. I chased me shaggin shoe up his arse. He was black and shaggin blue by de time Moriarty got to de house!'

'Are you not worried about him being in the Joy after your experiences in there Bins?' Siobhan asked.

'I tell ye Siobhan, better he has somptin else up his arse than be dead in the gutter, He's safer in der den on de streets. I warned him, I beat de shaggin shite outta him, I told him a million times I'm not having dat shite in de house around de young ones.'

Bins looked behind himself again.

'How's Maggie taking it?' Siobhan asked him.

'Sher, I had to give her clip to shurrherup. The shaggin shoutin and screaming when I phoned Garda Moriarty. Half de estate heard her. I tell ye Siobhan, how'd it look when the gang of us is out dere day after day breaking the arms of de shaggin dealers, and me own son is one of dem?

'Wha kindafa man would I look? De whole estate ud be laughin at me. Feck him. I don't want to talk abouh him anymore. What's happened has happened. It's his own shaggin fault.'

Siobhan could understand very well that Bins had found himself between a rock and a hard place. He was in a state of anger and emotional confusion. He had been forced to make a decision. To grass-up his own son, was against any rule of the culture Bins inhabited. The only other choice he had was to let Martin die. Hopefully Martin might make use of the drug-rehab program recently started in the Joy.

'How's Eamon, Bins, Did he get over his cold?'

'Ah sure don't talk to me about tha one.

'Why?' Siobhan said.

Bins looked at Siobhan, then behind him. 'Didn't he come home from school and announce he was going to make his First Holy Communications!

'I told him, over my shaggin dead body ye are. And the next minute Maggie shouts from the kitchen. "Ah, sure at least let one of them make it!!"

'I tell ye Siobhan, she's getting too brave for her own good dat one. Only tha I'd been doing me breathin did she get away with dat!'

'I know how you feel about the church Bins, but how do you think young Eamon is going to feel, being the only one in his class not making his Holy Communion?' Siobhan challenged him.

Bins looked behind him and started to shout at her.

'I don't shaggin care. I went down to the church and had a go at dat shaggin Father Doherty.'

Siobhan's voice became quieter. 'I thought you wouldn't go into the church?' she challenged him again.

'I shaggin didn't. I shouted for yer man to come out. I told him, youse lot had me where ye shaggin wanted me ye dirty feckers.

Yer not havin any son o mine in yer doirty club, youse can feck off.'

'What did he say?' Siobhan responded.

'He told me I was a hard man and dat I'd destroy me family before I finished. I shaggin reminded him dat his shaggin lot destroyed me. I tell ya Siobhan if dat shaggin lot offer me less than two hundred thousand in compo, I'll shaggin cut me wrists on the steps of the Doyle.

'Dey took me life, now dey can have me shaggin blood. What de ye tink Siobhan?'

'About what Bins?' Siobhan didn't know whether Bins was asking her opinion on the shouting match between him and the priest, outside the church; or the option of him cutting his wrists outside the Dail.

'About de compensation. How much de ye think we'll get? Will we get enough to go and live in a hot country, outta this shaggin place?'

'I don't know Bins it depends in which category you fall.'

Bins looked confused. 'What's dat mean?'

'Well,' Siobhan said. 'They do not seem to be sure yet. There is talk about categorizing. In other words Bins, they are going to put people into groups. Those who have been verbally abused and had the odd clip. Those that have been verbally abused and beaten. Those that have been emotionally, sexually and physically abused. You would come into that category Bins. Of course each Institution was different.'

Bins looked behind him, and then at Siobhan, he had not understood a word she had said. 'Categorize,' he thought, 'what the hell dez that mean? I'll have te start comin here with a shaggin dictionary under me arm.

'Sure I know they were different. Jesus, wasn't I in three of dem? Sure dey were all shaggin bastards.'

Siobhan slipped her pendant to the diamond side and asked Bins if he would like to do his breathing with her. Realizing he was getting to the point of exploding, he agreed. He looked behind him to check if he was safe, and then closed his eyes.

They sat for a few minutes inhaling and exhaling together. When Bins breathing reached the placid level of her own, his eyes opened and he had passed the crisis point.

'You know Bins,' Siobhan said. 'This compensation process could take years. I think it's, better if you can, to concentrate on your day to day life, living in the present. If you can make the present more comfortable for yourself, then you'll be able to cope with the future when it comes.'

Bins voice became calmer.

'Yer right Siobhan. I'm trying to cope, it's dis shaggin temper of mine, I just lose de head.'

'It's about losing control Bins, you still have to be in control of everything, don't you?'

'Well I'm not letting any other shagger control me Siobhan. There is no shaggin way, I tell ya dat fer free, No shaggin way!'

'Bins,' Siobhan said, 'you are letting your experiences of the past control you.

'You're a man now. No one can push you around and make you do things you don't want to do. You don't have to beat the crap out of everyone that disagrees with you Bins, especially the children. You are doing the same to them that they did to you. Those memories are controlling you, instead of you controlling them.'

Bins was quiet, he didn't respond. He knew she was right, but how the hell could he change himself, he thought?

'Look at Martin.' Siobhan continued, 'did the terrible beatings you gave him stop him going on drugs?'

'No,' Bins replied and looked behind him.

'Did you ever think he might be on the drugs because of the beatings?'

'Ah for God's sake don't be pulling that one on me Siobhan.'

'Did the beatings you had stop you ending up in the Joy?' Siobhan asked him.

'No,' he replied.

'No they made you sadder, angrier and more irrational. They also made you out of control. When you're out of control, the system takes over and your choices are taken away from you.'

Bins interrupted her, shouting.

'Nobody shaggin controls me.'

'Is that so?' Siobhan said. 'Well who was in control when you were locked up in the Joy, because you weren't?'

'I shaggin was,' he shouted.

Siobhan would not let go of Bin's irrational belief, his warped view of control needed to be challenged, and challenge it she would.

'No Bins, the prison officers were in control. The Warden was in control and some of the stronger inmates were in control.

'Perhaps Martin takes the drugs because he wants to forget what you are doing to him. Perhaps it eases his pain. Or perhaps he does it to get your attention, even though it earns him another beating!'

Bins sat quietly listening to her. Some of it made sense, he thought, but some of it was bollix.

'I don't know Siobhan. Are ya sayin that Martin is a druggy because I beat the shite outta him? I didn't buy him the skag. He shaggin stole from his mudder's purse and sold the shaggin television from under me nose to get it. Are ya sayin that beatins made him a druggy? Sher if dats true I'm de one who should be a druggy, no one was beaten more den me self! Are you sayin that if I keep beatin the udders to get some kinda of control in me own house, they'll become druggy's too?'

'What the shaggin feck are ya saying?'

They sat looking at each other. Bins face was distorted with anger. Siobhan faced his glare steadily, showing no sign of fear. It was not a confrontation. It wasn't a battle. It was a face-to-face challenge.

Siobhan had thrown down the gauntlet, exploiting and exploring Bins distorted belief that if he beat the shite out of everyone who looked at him sideways, it made him 'in control.'

'Who are you angry with right now Bins?'

'No one. I'm not shaggin angry!' he shouted, and looked behind him.

Siobhan didn't react.

'There is a crack in his hostility,' she thought. 'If only he'd had a bloody education in those institutions, he would have a vocabulary. If his reading skills are that of a six year old, how the hell can he vocalize his feelings? He does what a child does, lashes out physically. All his role models were sadistic, bullying bastards and he has taken on the same role with his kids.

'She doesn't understand,' Bins thought. 'How could she understand me? Alright fer her to talk, probably born with one of dem shaggin gold spoons in her shaggin gob.

'If I stop hitten and shoutin at the young ones Siobhan, will they grow up normal like?'

'I cannot predict that Bins, but I do know it is a good possibility that if you don't try harder to get your anger under control, you're going to have the rest of them on the Skag.'

'What'll I do Siobhan? Will I go to the anger management or wha?'

'I'm not even sure you're ready for that,' Siobhan said.

'It's run by two women. The last thing I need is for you to beat them up when they challenge you.'

'When did I ever hit a woman?' Bins shouted back at her.

'Get real Bins; you give Maggie a slap every week.'

'She doesn't count!' he replied and looked behind him.

'She knows what I'm like. I can control me self when I do the breathin and I'm happy when I go into me self hypnotics.'

'If you did your breathing as soon as you feel the anger starting, you'd be in control,' Siobhan said.

'Let me tell you Bins, every time you lose control; they're in control. Because your anger is the side-effect of what 'they' did to you. You've improved a lot the last two years but there is still a long way to go. However, if you do not start doing the homework I give you every week, there is not much point in continuing.

'One hour in therapy a week allows you to think about ways to help change your life. Unless you put the changes into practice when you leave here, nothing will change.

'You're wasting your time and mine.'

Bins looked behind him once more. 'Sorry Siobhan.'

He slapped himself on the forehead. 'I just shaggin forget everything when I leave here!'

'I'll give you a pad of Post It's and two pens, one red and one black,' Siobhan said.

'Jesus,' Bins thought, 'she's going to ask me to write a shaggin novel now!'

'All you have to do is write on them, "I'm in control, breathe." Or, "don't raise my voice," or "don't raise my hand." Write whatever warnings to yourself you want, you know the danger signals. Then stick them all over the house where you will see them. When you do see them go into your breathing straight away to calm you down.'

Bins looked behind him, then at Siobhan. 'Maggie will think I've shaggin lost it if she sees them things.'

'We are talking about anger-management here Bins, "managing your anger."'

'Tell her first what you are going to do. Communicate with her Bins; she is not a mind-reader. Ask her to remind you to breathe, I am sure she would be glad you were doing something about your problem.

'Where would you put the first sticker?'

Bins looks behind himself and shrugged his shoulders.

'What do you do when you get out of bed in the morning, I mean out from under the bed?' Siobhan asked him.

'I go and have a piss.'

'Okay, stick one on the bathroom mirror.'

'No the best place would be up on the wall over the toilet. Then when I stand on the chair to piss I can see it.'

'Okay,' she said. 'What will you write on it and what color pen will you use?'

Bins think for a minute.

'I'll write, "SMILE SIOBHAN IS WATCHING ME" in red. Does it matter about me shaggin spelling?'

'No of course it doesn't, as long as you understand what you write. Good, great, now you are thinking, and starting to manage your anger… and, that makes you 'in control.' What about the next one, where will you put that?

'I'll put that one the over the sink.'

'Why?' asked Siobhan.

'Because when I have a piss I always wash me hands and face and brush me teeth.'

'That is brilliant Bins, now you have it. Put the stickers up all over the house, they will be a constant reminder for you that you are in control, not out of control. Perhaps you could just write two words on a few of them, such as "STOP, BREATHE". That will remind you to do your breathing, which will calm you down.'

Bins was delighted with himself. 'I'll do this, he thought; I'll be in control, even if I have to plaster the whole house and the shaggin street wid dem things!'

'I wanted to ask you something Siobhan.'

'What is it Bins?'

'I was going through a bin over in Skerries before it went onto the truck. And I found a plastic bag with some jewellery in it. It's the real stuff Siobhan, and I'm in two minds whether to hand it in, or fence-it. What do you think?'

'Could you not take it back to the house where you found it?' Siobhan asked.

'Well ya see Siobhan, that's the problem, it wasn't a house. It was one of dem shaggin posh estates with dem electric gates. It has de big bins dey all put their rubbish in.

'You know how I jump into dem and have a bit of a root before dey they go on the truck? Well there it was and it just jumped into me hands with a frozen chicken! I think somebody must have cleaned out their freezer and forgot dey hid their jewellery there!'

'What do you think you ought to do Bins?' Siobhan asked.

Bins looked behind, as if to make sure no one was listening. 'Well a bit of me tinks it's fate and we could do with de money. And de udder bit tinks "Maggie ud love it". And den a bit of me tinks some poor ould biddy is crying her eyes out and lookin everywhere for it. What de ya tink?'

Siobhan looked at bins. 'Your decision Bins.'

'Ah sure, shag it,' Bins replied.

'What ya don't have ya can't miss. I'll give it to Garda Moriarty.'

'I think that's a very wise decision Bins. Or, next time you go there you could put up a note on the gate saying, "jewellery found" and put your phone number on it. If anyone rings you, ask them to describe the jewellery. Once you are sure, it is the rightful owner, make arrangements to return it. I am sure they would be extremely happy and like to thank you in person.'

'Sher that's a great idea Siobhan, why didn't I tink of dat? Ah well, dat's dat, I suppose.'

Siobhan asked him if had thought any more about joining the Group.

'To tell ya the honest ta God truth Siobhan, I don't like de idea of it much but I'll try it once and see how it goes.'

'Well done Bins, that's two good decisions you've made today. You should be proud of yourself. By the way are you going to the Joy to visit Martin?'

'I don't want to really. Maggie went de udder day and dere was no talkin to her after it. She called me every name under de sun. I threatened to ring up Child-Line if she didn't shut her gob.'

'Child-Line is for children Bins!'

'Sher don't I know dat Siobhan, sher how would they know what age I am?

'Okay so Siobhan, I'll see ya soon, please God.'

Siobhan opened all the windows before she walked into the garden. She lay on the warm grass beside a sculptured, granite, statue of a child. The child was looking down, clasping a bowl with his little hands. Water was flowing into the bowl and the overflow trickled into a small pool. Closing her eyes, she allowed the sound to clear her brain and wash away the tension from her body.

She thought of Bins. He collects garbage, and a like a piece of garbage the system spewed him out, but unlike garbage, you cannot recycle a damaged child.

What did he do? Stole a bicycle when he was seven, could not even ride the thing! Eight years he spent being tossed and dumped between various institutions, and the cycle goes on. Martin's in the Joy and we have the rest of his kids being indoctrinated with the violence, all the preparation in place to follow in their father's footsteps.

Once her inner conversation ceased she relaxed and gave her body and mind up to the sun and the sound of the water.

Chapter 7

TOM WAITED at the end of the drive. He glanced at his watch. 'One minute thirty two seconds to go,' he said to himself.

Thomas was never late for his appointments with Siobhan. If he was early he would wait patiently. He would never dream of knocking on Siobhan's door until it was the precise time.

Siobhan watched him from the window; she appreciated his timing and his respect. Some clients had to learn that being early or late for appointment was not appreciated. Silly excuses were not tolerated, their fifty minute sessions were as important for them as they were for her.

If they arrived ten minutes late and wasted more time complaining about traffic delays, she told them to leave their house an hour earlier. The time left was what they got and not a minute more.

Time for Siobhan was all about respect and self-discipline. Nothing annoyed her more than having to wait for an appointment with a medical consultant for herself. Many was the time she told them, her time was as important as theirs. She couldn't bear the arrogance of doctor's making a batch of appointments for 11am and keeping everyone waiting.

She noticed that though the day was warm, Tom still wore his Arsenal football scarf. His wife joked that Tom even wore it over his pajamas and always insisted on washing it by- hand himself. It had become his comfort blanket.

Siobhan had a special affinity with Tom. There was something trusting and childlike about him. She often felt like giving him a cuddle, patting him on the back and assuring him everything would be okay. Perhaps he brought out a dormant, maternal instinct in her. Always extremely aware of boundaries and ethics, she resisted the impulse. The only time she touched a client, was, if she needed to return a handshake.

'Good afternoon Tom, How are you today?'

Nn… not too bb…. bad thanks Siobhan.'

He smiled as he walked past her into the room. Siobhan always allowed her clients to choose their own seats. Tom always preferred the centre cushion of the three-seater settee.

It held a certain fascination for her, as to why, people continuously chose to sit in the same place. Very often, when she gave lectures, Siobhan would mischievously and at random, change the seating during the lunch-break.

The result was quite amazing. Students would look confused and a little uncertain when they returned to find their chair including their belongings in a different place. It discomforted them more when they realized they had new neighbours either side of them.

A simple change in the environment, which they had only inhabited for four hours made them feel unsafe.

Siobhan used this as an example to impress on her students, how it must feel to be a displaced person.'

'Imagine for a moment,' she would ask them. 'How a human-being feels. When through a natural disaster, such as an earthquake, tsunami, flood or fire, has destroyed everything you recognized as your own personal environment?'

After they answered that question, she would then ask them; how it would feel, if it was a man-made disaster such as a bomb!?

Her final question would be: 'Consider how a child would feel, if it was dragged out of his home, and away from all the familiarity of his family?'

This question usually elicited physical and emotional responses from both male and female students. As far as she was concerned, there was no place for complacency within the realms of trauma. Students needed to understand that they didn't need to experience trauma, they did need however, to have the ability to feel.

Tom was settled and comfortable.

'I own.... own only threw uuup once th... th... th... this week Sio... Siob Siobhan.'

Siobhan was used to Tom's stutter, she was patient and never had the urge to start, intervene or finish off his sentences for him.

'Well done Tom. What do you think triggered that one off?'

'We were sss.... staying at a bbb... bed and breakfast in Kilkil.... Killarney at th... th... the weekend, and th… they gave us porr… por… porridge for break breakfast. I did… didn't have to even put my fingers down my th… the throat, it just came up on its own.'

'Could you not have just asked for something else, instead of the porridge Tom?' Siobhan asked.

'Nn… no Siobhan. I… I was hope… hope… hoping Chrissie would do that ff… for me,' he replied.

Siobhan reminded him of his last session. 'Last week, when Chrissie came with you Tom, didn't we all agree that she would stop talking for you?'

Tom looked a little uncomfortable.

'We dd… did Siobhan, bb… but it's still dd… diff… diff… difficult for me to be arse.. arse… arsserertive.'

'Well it's a good start anyway Tom. Take a few deep breaths now and try to relax.'

Tom inhaled and exhaled.

'Funny,' he thought to himself, 'I never feel self-conscious doing this with Siobhan.' When Tom talked to himself, he didn't stutter. It always surprised him, when he was having a good natter to himself, especially when he was watching the football. Then Chrissie would interrupt by offering him a cup of tea? It would take him so long to get the 'yes' out, that Chrissie had come to issue warnings. Eventually she came to demand that he just nod or shake his head.

'That's better, Siobhan. It ww… was a bit of a rr… rush getting hh… here today, we spent too… too long in Bew… Bewleys!'

Siobhan smiled, she loved the way Tom and his wife Chrissie, used his appointments with her, as a day out. The full Irish breakfast in Bewleys and stroll down Grafton Street to the bus stop, was part of their routine.

'I hh… had me ch… ch… check-up at Beaumont the other d day Siobhan.'

'How did you get on Tom?' Siobhan asked.

'He said, "me… me back is a l… lot stro… stronger, b… but I n… need to do m… mor… more ex… exercises with me legs. I have to keep doing me psyc… psych… psyciltherapy."

Tom's stutter decreased, the more relaxed he became but his vocabulary was restricted, anything more than two syllables were impossible for him. It didn't worry him anymore, he simply went with the flow and made up his own words.

'Did he mean physiotherapy Tom?' Siobhan asked.

'Oh yes, th… that's what he said. I get them words muddled. Psychiltherapy is wh… wh… what I d… d… do with you isn't it?'

Siobhan had never corrected his lack of verbal skills. For her it was an irrelevant part of the work they did together. As long as they understood each other, Tom could relax.

'More or less.'

Siobhan sat serenely waiting for Tom to speak again.

'The kids were over fer… the E… E… Easter Siobhan, we ha… had one of th… them Bar and Qus on Sunday. It was a g… great day.' He sighed.

'I d… d… don't know how Chrissie man… managed, but the girls are great and they did did sum… some of those things on st… sticks, what are they c… call… called n… now? Kab… things. Anywayas whatever the for… for… foreign name is th… they were great.'

A slight frown creased his brow; Siobhan asked him if there was anything worrying him.

'I'm worried ab... ab... about that b... boy of Peadar's.'

'Is that young Sean, Tom?' Siobhan asked him.

'It is,' Tom replied.

'Why are you worried about him, you mentioned this before didn't you?'

'I th... think, I d... did Siobhan. Well he's w... wild. He never sits down. He runs him him... himself into the ground. God my n... nerves do be at me watching h... him. Sometimes when those l... l... little ones are around me. I have to g go and lock meself in the bb... bedroom for a bit of ab... break.

Anyway Peadar w... was saying he took him to the doc... doctor and the doctor said Sean was hype... hyp... hyp... hp... hypoeo... reactive. He said th... the child would set set... settle down b... by the t... time he goes to school and they were t... to be careful wh... wh... what f... food they gave him.

Why would th... that be Siobhan?'

'Well there are additives in some foods such as colourings Tom; they have an effect on some children. Take some sweets for instance, with all the different colors, those can make some children hyperactive. It means the child finds it difficult to sit still or concentrate.'

'I never s... s... saw a sweet till I w... was nearly fifteen Siobhan. I bought some wi... wi... with me first pay p... packet. The kids are v... v... very lucky th... these days. Thank God. I'm f... .... feeling much better n... n... now Siobhan since I told Chrissie and the k... kids.'

There was silence in the room. Siobhan smiled at Tom. He had been through so much. His whole life had been a nightmare. How he had managed to keep his secrets to himself for over forty years was unbelievable.

'It must be a lot easier for you now Tom,' Siobhan replied.

'I w... wi... wish I'd done it years ag... ago. They all und... d... erstand... now why I tried to kill meself.'

Tom was silent for a while. 'They're grand kid's s so they are. Chrissie did a grand job r... rearing them.

'Som... som... etimes... I wonder how she'd did it all and w... worked as well. And me like a lun... lunatic... hidin... all me life in a se... sewer.'

Tom sat in the chair looking like a lonely, sad child. Siobhan's heart went out to him.

'It was a job Tom,' Siobhan said. 'Please Tom; give yourself some credit and respect for holding down a job for forty-seven years. You even got promotion a few times. There aren't many that can do that.'

'I know th... that Siobhan. Yes it w... was a job, b... but it was a hiding place, a place where no one would know th... that I couldn't r... read or write. Imagine sp... spending nearly forty years cleaning u... up people's sh... sh... shit? All because I w... was ash... ashamed and fright frightened. A lifetime in a sewer. A lifetime trying t... to h... hide and r... run way f... from my my... own st... stup... stupid fears!'

Siobhan recognized the emotion in Tom's voice. His Adam's apple pressed against the scar on his throat.

'It wasn't your fault Tom,' Siobhan told him sternly. This isn't the time for self-blame.

'We talked about this so many times. Whose fault was it, whose responsibility was it?'

'Theirs,' Tom replied. 'It was all their fault.'

'Yes,' she said. 'They beat you, they force-fed you. They assaulted you and knocked your teeth out. What were you Tom?'

'The ch… ch… child, Siobhan. I was just a ch… ch… child. Do you know Siobhan, I can never see or feel myself like a child. When I looked at the grandkids m… mes… messin… and havin… a gr… great time at the weekend, I felt like c… c… cr… cryin!'

'Yes,' Siobhan said. 'That's understandable Tom. Childhood is all about exploring, learning, laughing, cuddles and kisses, being comfortable and safe and so much more.'

'I even f… f… ind… it difficult to pick up me grandkids. I don't even tt… think I ever kis… kised me own kids. Thank God Chrissie sm… sm… smothered them in kisses; she never left them alone come to think of it. There w… wasn't anything anyone of them asked ff… for and she didn't find a way t… to get it for them. When I think of the piano, g… gititar, trumpet and all th… them m… musical lessons th… they had, and how they can read all the m… music, and I can only read me o… oweown name, it's like a miracle what she did with them. Look at them when they get together? I… it's like having our own band. The voice on that Deidre is…. well she should be on the tele Siobhan.'

Siobhan smiled and agreed with him, Deirdre had a remarkable voice. Chrissie had brought in a tape of her singing Ave Maria and it was spell binding.

'Some t… times, I th… think of meself working in th… the l… leth… leather shop Siobhan. I can st… still smell those bit… bit… bits of leather! If they'd let me he... heel and sole a shoe, it might have been worth it. Mm... making those terrible leathers they used to beat the living daylights out of us, was a, a crime. A cr... crim... criminal thing to do to a child. Don't you th... think so Siobhan?'

Siobhan shivered involuntarily. She remembered the occasion one of her clients had brought in a 'leather' to show her. That particular one had discs, resembling coins embedded into the thongs.

'It was insane Tom,' Siobhan replied.

'Why do you think they took you out of your lessons and put you in the leather shop and then on the farm?'

'I d... d... don't know Siobhan, Sher... th... there was no sense in any... anything they'd did! I was too small to reach the at table and they made me st... stand on a box all day!'

'Ah J... Jayzus they kn... new I was t... terrified of the turkeys. Because I used t... to vom... vomit and nearly faint when they made me cut the t... turk... turkey's throat. Weren't they crazy t... to put a b... boy from the inner ci... cit... city to work on a bloo... bloody farm?'

Siobhan had various thoughts about the reason, the main answer being 'sadistic'. Nothing those animals did, made any sense at all. They sat in silence for a while. Tom reached for the glass of water on the table in front of him. He drank it in one go. Siobhan asked him if he would like another one.

'No no th... thanks Siobhan. I never r... re... realized how thirsty you get when you t... talk,' he said.

'I suppose b... be... cause I never bloody talked before. Ch... Chrissie used to complain, all I did was grunt. She used to say she was m... ma... m... married to a grunter. People u'd ask her "which part of the country was Grunt from?"'

He laughed and Siobhan smiled.

'She used t... t... to tell them it was in th... the West of I... Ir... Ireland!'

Tom sat for a moment examining his bitten fingernails, a habit he had never tried to correct.

'I think the worst mem... memory I have Siobhan is about Paddy. When he c... came out of that Brothers' office cr... cr... crying, with blood all over the back of his trousers. And running down his legs.

'I didn't know ww... what to do. I didn't kno... know how to save him from that bast... bastard. I c... couldn't p... pro... protect him.'

Tom's lower chin started to quiver, his voice broke, he reached into his pocket and took out a neatly ironed handkerchief.

'He never ev... ever spoke about it and I c... could not sp... speak about it either. But I'm sure th... that's why he killed himself!'

The sobs gradually stopped. Siobhan asked him if he would like to walk in the garden with her.

'That ud be l... lovely, may as well while we have a bit of sun today. Sher it might be r... raining tomorrow Siobhan.'

Tom picked up his scarf and wound it round his neck. He visibly relaxed as they entered the garden. He took in the scent of the lavender bush.

'It's a g… great job you've done here, Siobhan. You h… ha… have them green finger things. The same as my Chrissie.'

They sat down at the small hand carved table.

'It's a terrible th… thing to l lose a brother Siobhan. It's ev… even w… worse to lose a twin. I do… don't think there was ever a d… day since th… th… the day Paddy came out of that off… off… office, that I haven't thought about h… him.'

Tom's voice raised slightly. Siobhan believed Tom didn't have the ability to shout. He didn't even like loud noises.

'I could kill every last one of them Siobhan. I c… c… could c… cut their throats, like I did the tur… turkeys Siobhan. Now I know how to let me a… an… anger out I feel much better. Even me stut… stutter is better. You know Chrissie is delighted with me progress?'

'That's good?'

'Yes she can't believe I can act actually hold a convers… conversation for fifteen minutes. She started to time me when I start talking.' Tom laughed.

'She got one of th… those stop cock watch things from Argus. And she reminds me ev… every time I shut down and stop listening.

'She shouts "you've switched off again, so you have you oweled eejit you."'

Tom laughed and Siobhan joined in.

'She's a clever woman Tom,' Siobhan remarked.

'The best s… so she is, the best. Ah sure I don't know what I'd d… do without her. She's one of the best. In f… f… fact she is the b… b… best! I'll n…

never forgive m… me self for putting her through all of that Siobhan.

'Did I tell you Siobhan, the k… kids bought us a trip to b… Blackpool for our anniversary?'

'No you didn't Tom,' Siobhan replied.

'Yes,' Tom said. 'A a… l… lo… long weekend, in a five s… s… star hotel, isn't that grand Sh… Siobhan?'

'That's wonderful Tom, are you looking forward to it?' Siobhan asked.

'I am that Siobhan. I've never been in a five star hotel! Chrissie and I always took the kids to a caravan. They could r… run as wild as they wanted and we didn't have to worry about disturbing other people. It w… was Ch… Chrissies time o… off and she wouldn't cook. We ate at the chippie every night! The k… k… kids loved it.

'Ye know Siobhan, in all th… those years I worked in the se… sewers, I never took a drink. Is isn't that s strange?'

'Never?' Siobhan asked.

'No. Never,' Tom replied.

The oth… other l lads 'ud go off to one of the pubs th… that op… opened early in the mo… morning, but I'd ju… just g… go straight h… home.

I ne… never eve… en… took a drink at my Paddy's f… f… funeral. God rest his soul.

Maybe I sh… sh… should have got drunk a f… few times.'

'Why do you say that Tom?' Siobhan asked.

Tom shrugged his shoulders and thought for a while.

'Well it might have made me forget what happened to me. I wish I'd known th… then how to do me hypnosis.'

'The trouble with the drink Tom,' Siobhan said, 'is it might make you forget for a little while, but the side-effect would be depression and the likelihood of you having to drink more and more to forget.'

'Yeah, I seen enough of me Da falling a... around the pl... place wh... when he to... took up the drink. Do ye think they drink because they're trying to forget or are b... because they're depressed like I wa... was?'

'It's difficult to say Tom. I am not sure if people are depressed so they drink, or people are depressed because they drink .I do know the two go hand-in-hand. Alcohol abuse in this country is endemic; it appears to most people to be the norm. Just be happy you never started it Tom. Believe me it would have made your problems a hundred times worse.'

'End... end... endemic, th... th... that's a big work Sh... Siobhan. Al almost as big as marm... marmalade!'

Both of them laughed.

'How do you feel now Tom?' she asked him.

'Ah sure I f... f... feel grand, l... like I always do when I c... come here and have a chat with you Sh... sh... Siobhan.'

'Good, I think your stutter is improving Tom, What about the speech therapist, did you think anymore about going to see her?'

'I did. Ch... Chr... Chrissie and I talked it over and as she says she's used to me stuttering all ov... over the place. And did I want to be a fec... fec... fecking politician or wha? I told her I'm a stut stutterer not a feckin liar!'

Siobhan laughed and clapped her hands. 'Well done Chrissie,' she said. 'That's okay Tom, it's your decision, and as long as you are happy that's the most important thing. What about the group, did you talk that over with Chrissie?

'I did. Chrissie thinks it would be good for me.'

Tom looked a little unsure of himself; he

was a shy man. Siobhan worried he might feel a little overpowered in a group situation.

'Yes, but how do you feel about it Tom?' Siobhan asked.

'Well I sup… suppose I'm a bit nerv… nervous about it. But I'll give it a go. As long as you are around I'll be fine.'

'Good man,' Siobhan praised him. 'What are your plans for the rest of the day Tom?'

As Tom stood up, he wrapped his Arsenal scarf around his neck and patted it in place.

'Well I'm going to meet Chrissie, she's down the road, in Primark, looking for bargains as usual. Imagine, there's never a day when she doesn't find s… something half-price fo… for either birthday or Ch… Christmas presents for all the grandkids. She even buys all the Christmas paper and c… cards after Christmas cause they are so cheap. The problem is she can never find them eleven months later. Then we're going to a concert in the St Stephen's pp… park. She's made a few s… sandwiches and a flask of tea.'

'Lovely idea Tom, enjoy it and make the most of the sunshine.'

'We will Sh… Siobhan; thanks for your t… time and take care. See you at the Group then.'

Siobhan watched him walk down the drive. She noticed that he didn't drag his feet anymore. His step was also a lot lighter than it used to be. It took him a lifetime to come out of the shadows and into the light. Now he's like a child experiencing the delight of splashing through a puddle wearing a pair of new shoes. Everything we miss in childhood will eventually catch up with us, she thought.

He had endured forty years of silence, unspeakable brutality, and existed only within the boundaries of his own nightmares.

It had been a long day. Every day was a long day. Siobhan walked out into the garden and kicked her shoes off, one after the other they flew up into the air. This was one of the experiences she had missed as a child, the freedom to do it now never failed to delight her. She walked around the garden bare-foot and slipped out of her skirt, unbuttoned her blouse, shook it off her delicate shoulders and let it float to the ground.

Lying on the grass, cooled by the fading sun, she sighed, breathed deeply and exhaled, releasing all the pain her body and mind had absorbed that day. The sky was still blue above her head; just one patch of a cotton wool cloud hovered overhead.

In ten minutes she would shower and change her clothes obliterating any residue of the grief and anger bequeathed to her by her clients. Siobhan could not carry any of it home with her, it would be an invasion of her own personal space.

Chapter 8

SIOBHAN ALWAYS wore pastel shades, even at funerals. The majority of her clients, when they started consulting her, wore dark colors. Black, navy, brown. Gradually, as they progressed through their therapy the colors slowly changed. She always knew when clients were feeling happier with themselves. Not only the colors changed, they walked differently, they held themselves differently, their body language changed.

The women started to change their style of clothing, make-up and hair was re-vamped. Siobhan refused to use the phrase 'make-over.' For her clients, who had forgotten who they were, what they were, and how they were, they regained their identity. They had re-claimed the woman or man within. Unfortunately this was a long journey, very often they had to start at the beginning and claim their inner child first.

Siobhan hadn't seen clients that day. She had cleared and cleaned her consulting room.

A bunch of dried sage had been set alight, as soon as a flame had appeared she blew it out. Holding the sage in one hand, she swirled it around every wall, nook and cranny. Holding it high, the wisps of smoke swirled around the ceiling. Small containers of rock-salt placed in each corner of the room were disposed of and then renewed. Incense had been burned throughout the morning and removed during the afternoon. All the windows had been opened wide to allow the sickly aroma to escape.

Siobhan held the belief that a room held the pain of every emotion and disclosure brought into it.

Tonight was for the Group. Each and every one of them would bring in their own story, each and every one of them would own the room, and she didn't want any remnants from a day's work to defile the atmosphere.

Siobhan could hear the sound of voices outside and surprisingly some laughter, she looked at her watch and smiled.

'Any minute now,' she thought.

There was a gentle knock at the door; she opened it to see Gerard bowing gracefully, almost touching his head to his knees. She smiled.

'Good evening Gerard how are you?'

'Great Siobhan and how's yourself?' he said, grinning from ear to ear.

Tom followed behind Gerard.

'How are youth th… th… this evening Siobhan?' he said.

'Good thanks Tom, I see you've met Gerard.' 'I have so,' he replied.

A moment later, Ant appeared, holding his hand out to Siobhan, she shook it gently.

'How are you Ant?'

'Not too bad Siobhan,' he whispered to her, 'I went to the funeral.'

Siobhan nodded her head, smiled at him and whispered back, 'Good, I'm glad you did Ant.'

The men all chose their seats. Gerard and Tom sat on the settee, still talking to each other. Ant chose a chair nearest Siobhan, he appeared a little nervous.

Gerard smiled over at Ant.

'How are you, have we met somewhere before?'

'I don't think so,' he replied.

Bins walked through the open door.

'How're yes? How're ya Siobhan?'

'I'm very well thanks Bins, I'm glad you could come.'

Bins chose the seat facing the door, sitting down he briefly looked behind him and nodded to the others.

Cracker walked through the door and stopped; he pushed the door behind him, looked around at the other men and nodded his head briefly.

'How'r yez? How' r ye Siobhan?'

He rolled his eyes heavenwards looking at Siobhan, as if to say 'what the hell am I doing here?'

Siobhan smiled at him.

'Nice to see you Cracker.'

He grinned back at her. The door opened and Dezzie tentatively peeped around it, he paused for a moment as if wondering if he was in the right place.

'Come on in Dezzie, great you could come, have a seat.'

Dezzie chose a seat near Cracker, who did a sideways look at Dezzie's ponytail and rolled his eyes. Dezzie looked straight ahead.

Tom looked at Dezzie and smiled.

'How'r yuh?'

'Okay thank you, 'yr'self?

'Ah,' said Tom, I'm not too bad thanks.'

Just as Siobhan was about to speak the door opened again and Allan entered the room. He looked at Siobhan first.

'Good evening Siobhan how are you?'

'Very well thank you Allan, we were just about to start, I'm glad you could make it. Siobhan smiled at him.

Allan looked at the other men, nodded his head and said, 'good evening gentlemen, I hope I haven't delayed you.'

They all looked at Allan, and then at Siobhan. Gerard was the only one who spoke. 'Sher not at all, yer very welcome so you are.' Allan smiled at him and sat in the only chair available, even though Gerard had shoved Tom a bit up the settee to make room for him.

'Well,' said Siobhan, 'you're all very welcome. I appreciate you have all taken the time and the courage to come to this first meeting. I do realize and understand it is difficult for some of you to be here.

'This first meeting we're leaving open. I don't want to put a time-limit on it. This is simply to give all of you the chance to talk and be able to express your feelings. There are a couple of things I would like to mention.

'First of all, everything that is said within this room tonight is confidential.

'This means that once you leave through that door, you do not mention anything you have heard or seen, even to each other. All of you need to understand that this has to be a safe place, and the only way to keep it safe is with one word silence.

'Does anyone have any questions about this rule?'

They all murmured, 'no'.

Bins shifted in his chair, and looked behind him.

'Too shaggin right!'

All heads, including Siobhan's' turned to look at Bins, he looked behind himself again.

'The next point I want to make, is this,' said Siobhan.

'Listening, is an important part of what you are going to do here this evening, and it is something you will all learn. Listening isn't't just about hearing words, it's about body language. If you are uncomfortable with something being said, try to respect the speaker by not interrupting, or using your body in anyway which might show disapproval.

'I'm going to use the word compassion here.

'All of you are survivors, all of you have experienced horrendous child abuse but you have survived. There is no pain measurement scale in this room. The pain each one of you might feel, with a memory of an experience, others will feel differently.

'There is a slight chance you might experience a recovered memory, one which you have long forgotten. If you feel physically uncomfortable or think you are going to experience any anxiety just raise your hand.

'This is your group. My input will be minimal. I will only interrupt you if I feel a situation might be harmful or you need some guidance.

'It might be helpful to do a few minutes relaxation before we start. What do you think?'

The men all nodded in agreement.

Bins jumped up from his seat and lay down on the floor facing the door; he leaned on one elbow, looked behind him, then settled down.

Gerard leaned back in his seat, spreads his long legs out in front of him, closed his eyes and started to breathe deeply, exhaling noisily.

Ant stroked his beard, stretched his arms upwards, yawned and closed his eyes. Tom folded his arms sat back on the settee and closed his eyes.

Dezzie shifted in his chair and tried to bring his knees up into the fetal position then closed his eyes. Allan looked straight ahead.

After viewing all of them Cracker rolled his eyes up to Heaven, sat up straight, put his head down, his hands relaxed on the arms of the chair.

There was silence, they opened their eyes again and looked at Siobhan, she placed her forefinger slightly under her diamond pendant. All with the exception of Allan closed their eyes again.

'When you are ready to come back you will feel relaxed and happy, just take your time. Three, two, one when you are ready open your eyes.'

Slowly the men opened their eyes; they sat up, stretched their limbs and smiled at each other.

'Cracker. How do you feel?' Siobhan asked.

Cracker puffed up with pride, delighted he was the only one singled out for attention.

'Great Siobhan, fuckin great!'

'Okay, so who is going to start the ball rolling?' Siobhan said, looking around at them all, but no one in particular.

The men looked at each other shyly. Dezzie appeared intimidated, hanging his head and trying to become invisible. Gerard then spoke.

'Right so. I'm Gerard and I'm an alcoholic. I've been in recovery for over ten years but I'm still a feckin alcoholic. Now lads let me tell ya.....'

He was interrupted by Siobhan, her hand slightly raised, leaning forward in her chair.

'Gerard, just to remind you, this isn't' an AA meeting! Okay?'

Gerard laughed.

'Jaysus, will ya listen to me, I don't know how to talk unless I have a feckin podium and an audience! Ya see it's the addickidtion. I got to understand me addickidtion problem through Siobhan. There was no addickter in me family so it wasn't genius, ye know wha I mean, it didn't't come down through me trousers like?'

He looked at Siobhan for confirmation.

'Is it me trousers or me jeans Siobhan? '

'Genes, Gerard,' Siobhan replied.

Tom, and Bins looked confused, Cracker and Ant smiled, Dezzie kept his head lowered. Allan looked as if nothing abnormal had been said.

'Anywayas, I suppose it all started when I was around eight. Me father had just died and me mother would have frightened the shite out of an elephant God rest her soul.

'Now I was a big lad and me mother was only four foot seven; but I tell you there was no better woman that could pick up a broom handle and break it over your back, before you could say 'feckin!'

'Anywayas I got caught mitchin from school and stealin a bag of sweets. Me mother stood up for me in court, but the judge said I was out of control. Me mother started to shout at the judge about how many handles she'd broken over me back, so how could I've been out of control? "Sure wasn't he only mitchin from the school yer judgeship," she said.

'"Ye mustta done that yerself at one time or another, sure doesn't every young kid do that. The sweets were just a small bag of Jelly Beans, sher what harm is that?"

'Anywayas didn't the oeld shite sentence me to Marlborough Howese and from there I was sent to Upton.'

Bins interrupted talking loudly through his nose. 'Ah Jayzus dat shaggin concentration camp!' He looked behind him.

'It was that,' Gerard said, 'I say, it was that.

'Anywayas, wasn't I very tall for me age, the younger lads the same age as me self were terrified of me. The oewelder lads were so rough, they were a feckin Mafia and I was terrified of them. After all it was the first time I'd ever been away from me mammy.'

All except Cracker, Ant and Allan nodded with silent support. Ant looked at Gerard calmly with total concentration, Cracker rolled his eyes to heaven and Allan's face showed no emotion.

'Well after a few days some of them oewelder lads came up te me and towelled me I had to be eider with them or against them. Sure what was I goin to say te that? I told them I was with them.

'They said I had to go troo an inspiration test, now I hadn't a feckin clue wha they were talking about and said "okay" so. Didn't they take me inta the toilets and made me do, well yez know yerselve,s I'm fuckin sure what went on in them toilets. Jayzus and to think, up until then I thought me willie was just for pissing!'

Bins interrupted Gerard again. 'Ah sure don't ya know?' Bins looked behind himself, as if he wasn't sure he had looked behind him, he repeated the movement.

'Well I feckin sure found out, I tell you. Between the oulder fellas and them Rosminians, there wasn't a day went by where I didn't go to bed crying and calling for me mammy. Six of those Rosminians laid in ta me one night with their leathers, and in the morning I woke up stuck to the feckin sheets with the blood, so I did.'

Bins interrupted again.

'Ah sure, don't ya know?'

Siobhan looked at Bins and quietly told him to try not to interrupt Gerard whilst assuring Bins that he would have plenty of time to have his say later.

'Right so Siobhan. Gerron with it then Ger,' Bins said.

'Well as I was saying, a lot of terrible things went on in that godforsaken place. Because I was a tall fellah they made me join the boxing team. Well I tell ya, the little fellahs were running away from me in the ring and I was more scared of them, shitting meself I was, and running in the opposite direction. I might have looked like Casius Clay, but sure I felt like Minnie feckin Mouse.'

All of them started to laugh and Gerard joining in the laughter stood up and started to mimic himself in a boxing ring; running away with his knees high and his arms pumping up and down.

The only one who didn't laugh was Dezzie.

The tension in the room lifted as Gerard enjoyed his moment of fame.

Gerard continued: 'I'm a tap dancer you see, always tapped me way around everything, so I stuck drawing pins in me shoes and tapped me way around the ring, I was like feckin Fred Upstairs, so I was. Sure after a year or so I jumped over the feckin wall and ran away.

'I hadn't a feckin clue where I was! I joined a crowd walking into a grave-yard. I pretended I was part of the family of the dead person. 'Then I made a mistake pretending to cry for me aunty and someone said it was me uncle!

'I followed them to the pub and ate meself stupid I was that hungry.

'That was when I got a taste for the drink. Someone put a Guinness in me hand and someone else put a Jamison's in me other hand. There was a fellah playing a jig on the accordion and I started me tap dance. Well everyone had a few jars on them and they were clapping and singing. Then I lost the run of meself with the drink like and jumped on a table. Next thing I knew was waking up in the hospital with two broken legs and fractured ribs. I gave the nurse me cousin's name and had a job remembering I was Billy not Gerard.'

All the men started laughing again, even Dezzie was sitting up straight in his chair laughing.

Gerard was on a roll, he loved entertaining.

'Ah Jayzus,' he said, 'I loved it in there. Have yez ever had a bed bath?

All of them shook their heads.

'Ah Jayzus, you don't know what yez are missing. You lie in the bed and a lovely nurse has a bowl of water and a bit of soap and an old flannel, she gives you a wash and dry all over. Now I was never one fer a bit of water. Me mammy, God rest her soul, used to cut the arse off me trying to catch me to get into the old tin bath. I tell yez, I couldn't't get enough of those bed baths, neither could me willie.'

The men all started laughing again.

'Mind you,' said Gerard, 'there was one drawback to that place. Nearly everyone in there was a geriatrix, and there was one ould fella who'd come up to me bed every night, and asked me to shake hands with his willie!

'Sure I didn't't want to offend the poor bastard so I did!'

Tom and Allan fell about laughing, Cracker had to hold his stomach, Siobhan had never seen Cracker convulsed with laughter. Bins kept laughing and looking behind himself, Ant and Dezzie smiled.

'Anyways,' Gerard continued, 'I was discharged, they sent me home and me mother sent me off to me sister's house to hide. I didn't't get on with me brother-in-law and one night we had a fight, I stole ten pounds from the bastard and I left the house.

'I went into the off-license and bought a half bottle of Jameson's and a couple of cans of Guinness and went down to the Quayside. I sat there with me legs dangling over the water, thinking I could jump a boat to England, or hide on one of them cruise boats and end up on a desert island or something. I finished me cans and whisky, stood up, but I was pissed and missed me footing and fell in the feckin Liffy.

'That wouldn't't have been so bad if I could've swam!'

Tom broke the silence.

'JJ… Jesus Gerr… aren'd, you l… lucky to be here to tell the tale ss… so you are!

'Ah sure don't you know Tom? Me and me bad luck go hand in hand. A couple of Gardai from Sherif Street were passing by; they dragged me out with a bit of oweld rope and then arrested me for being a runner.

I was trying to tell them what was happenin to me in that place and they kept giving me a clip on the ear and said "I was a drunkin liar eejit". They threw me into a cell and the next day took me up to the court and didn't't I get the very same judge who had sent me to feckin Upton!

'Me mammy was there again and this time she brought the handle of the brush with her, to prove to the judge how she could control me.

'The feckin judge told her I needed a ball and chain, not a brush handle and sent me off to Artane.

'Ah now out of the shagging fire!' said Bins, looking behind him. Siobhan looked at him, he ignored her.

'Anywayas,' Gerad said, 'I had woirser problems there. Didn't't they put me on the farm! Imagine putting a boy from Sherif Street on a feckin farm? Well I suppose I wasn't really on the farm. I was shoveling shite outta the feckin cow shed. I mean ta say, they were meant to educate us, where would ya find a feckin cow shed in Sherif Street for God's sake? What skills was that goin to give me?

'Anywayas, then I had a bit of luck, didn't I get the mumps and they put a bed in the cellar, and told me

I had to stay there. I tell ya there was feckin spiders in there as big as me fist. I used ta scream with the fright. Every time they heard me scream, they'd come and beat the shite outta me with the feckin leather.

'Then one night I was screaming with the fright and one of them bastards came down. 'A big fellah he was, with feckin orange hair, I think his name was Brother McGowan. He brought two of his henchmen with him.

'Well they laid inta me with their fists and boots. Then they finished me off with the leather. I didn't't remember anything 'till I woke up in the hospital two days later. I hadda broken nose and stitches in me lips and half me teeth were gone. The skin was ripped off me back and I was black and feckin blue and purple and yellow, in fact I was like a feckin rainbow.'

Tom became emotional and reached for a tissue to wipe his eyes. Siobhan looked at him.

'Are you okay Tom?'

Tom nodded his head.

'Anywayas thank God,' Gerard said, 'those bastards beat the shite outta me, because they signed me out of Artane, and I went home to me mammy.'

The men were all quiet, each one reflecting on the emotional, physical and degrading experiences Gerard had suffered.

'Ah sure there's load more so, but I had bad luck and no sense. I thought I was Al Capone. Me and the lads went out one night and decided to rob the off license.

'Sure we were feckin eejits; we only had one balaclava and a water pistol between us. Sure we didn't't take any money only a few ould cigarettes and a couple of bottles of Jameson.

We went to an old shed on the allotment and drank the lot, woke up in a heap on top of each other with yer man still wearing the balaclava.

'Anywayas I thought it was time I got meself out of Ireland. Me mammy gave me the money for the ticket and I got the mail boat over ta England. Well now you know why I became addickited to everything, because of me childhood experiences.'

There was silence in the room. Tom, looking visibly upset, his hands shaking, managed to pour himself a glass of water. Cracker wiped beads of sweat off his forehead. Dezzie bit his fingernails. Ant sat passively staring at the ceiling. Allan was quiet and reflective.

Siobhan then spoke.

'Thank you Gerard for sharing your experiences with us all. May I ask you a question?'

'Fire away Siobhan,' he replied.

'When you grew up, did you ever talk about your experiences in Upton or Artane?'

'I did in me feckin arse Siobhan. Sure didn't the guards beat the shite outta me the time I talked about it? Who would have believed me?

'I didn't' tell anything 'till the day I walked in here. Then I couldn't't believe me self, half the time, wondering, if I imagined it all. But I tell ya, I can still see that fecker McGowan's face. That bastard nearly killed me. I still wake up in the night screamin and roarin with the nightmares. Ever since that night I've hated orange hair. If I see anyone, a man or a woman with that kindda hair I want to feckin kill them!'

Cracker noisily cleared his throat.

'I know that fucker!' he said.

They all looked at Cracker.

'Oh I know that fucker very well, He hasn't't got the hair any more, it's white now. He's still got that fuckin evil face and that smell about him. Do you remember the smell Ger?'

'I do that Cracker, a kindda sweat and rotten teeth smell,' he replied.

'Mmm,' Cracker agreed.

Cracker looked at Siobhan, as if to say, 'I told you so!'

'Do you want to talk Cracker?' Siobhan asked.

'I might as well.'

Cracker reached over the table and poured himself a glass of water, wiped the sweat from his face and took a sip.

'Well, I met Siobhan two years ago; I was in the Joy, on remand for GBH. Me solicitor brought her in to prove I was fuckin nuts! It wasn't my fuckin fault I've never given the first slap in me life, those fuckers deserved it. Let me tell yez what happened.

'I was out this night having a few jars with some friends of mine and one of them suggested we go to a club in Parnell Street. The bastard said there was easy women to pick up there and sure ye know what it's like yourselves, a few jars and you don't care which fireplace you poke.

'Well, as I said I'd had a good few jars on me by the time we got there. I was chatting up this fine, looking woman when three lads jumped me from behind and dragged me out to an alley. Anyway the long and the short of it was I lost the fuckin head and beat the shite out of them.

'Then the Garda accused me of gay bashing, I nearly lost the head again, I wouldn't dirty me hands on a gay let alone give him a bash. How was I to know we were in a gay club and the bitch I was chatting up was a fellah? Jayzus I tell ye it'll be a long time before I go to a club again.

'Anyways, me solicitor told me I'd be going down for a good stretch this time. I don't mind doing time, it's the being closed in, that does me fuckin head in 'cause I'm claustro- bloody phobic.

'Anyways Siobhan pulled a load of shite out of me head that I'd never told anyone in me life. She stood up in court for me and the judge was nearly crying, and me self was crying too, it was like she was talking about someone else, not me.

'So yer man, the judge, believed I was acting in self-defense and there were extenuating circumstances; he gave me a fine to cover the bastards medical costs, probation and ordered me to sort out me fuckin head or else!

'I tell yez the law in this country is an arsehole. Because I work in security I'm not allowed to give anyone a flick, let alone a slap.'

'Ah so don't you know?' interrupted Bins, as he looked behind him.

Cracker continued.

'There were three of us when me mother died, meself, me brother and me sister. I was the youngest. We didn't't have much but we were wild and happy.

'We had a two room cottage on a farm me father used to work on down in Wexford, and we'd play out in the fields from morning till night. When we were hungry we'd run home for a piece of bread and drippin'.'

The men smiled. Each one of them had a memory of a large slab of bread slathered in dripping.

'I remember I was always the Lone Ranger, me brother was an Apache and me sister a Squaw. I'll never forget her. She had a thick, long black plait that ran half way down her back. Eyes that sparkled when she laughed and she was always giving me dribbly kisses down the back of me neck.

'They'd make bows and arrows from branches and a bit of ould string, and I'd shoot them with an ould water pistol. Many's the time they'd gang up on me, tie me to a fuckin tree and go home. I tell ye nobody I'd miss me 'till the big pot of potatoes went on the table, and then me mother I'd say, "where's Norman?" That's me real name. I hate it!

'I remember the day me mother died,' he paused for a minute before continuing.

'She wasn't sick, she wasn't you know, in the hospital or anything. She just didn't wake up one morning.

'I don't remember much after that except a big black car coming to the house and me and me brother being dragged out of the house kickin, screaming and shouting, "save us daddy, save us daddy." I remember the tears running down me daddy's face as he stood at the door.'

Cracker became emotional, put his head in his hands, and murmured.

'That was the end of me childhood. I was dragged out of the car in front of a big building, Goldenbridge it was, and then it took off again with me brother, it was the last I seen of him for a good few years.

'A fat smelly nun with a hood on her head dragged me kickin and screaming in to the building, I was terrified.'

Cracker shook his head.

'Jayzus what a place for a kid to be.

'Another big bully of a nun came and between the two of them they dragged me inta a bathroom, tore the clothes off me back and threw me into a bath of steaming water.

'I nearly died, I thought I was going to be boiled alive. They nearly took the skin off me with the fuckin scrubbin brush they used on me.

'I never forgot it. To this day I can't stand the smell of Dettol or anything like that, and I have a terrible fear of baths, I only use a shower, and if I'm somewhere there isn't't a shower, I use a bucket of water.'

Bins looked behind him and interrupted.

'Ah sure, don't ya know?'

The others ignored him and kept their eyes on Cracker.

'Fuckin bitches, evil, dirty bitches, so they were. Ye couldn't look sideways without getting a crack across the face, or yer ear nearly torn off. Sure it wasn't until years later did I realize that I couldn't look anyone in the face. Of course I couldn't', sher I was terrified I'd get a punch, that's what those bitches taught me.

'Every fuckin Friday they'd make us line-up and drop our trousers. If we had a mark of shite on our drawers they'd batter the living daylights outta us.

'For fucks sake, we only got clean drawers once a fortnight and half the time there was no toilet paper. What did they expect us to do, wipe our arses on the grass?'

'It was the same in Upton, Cracker,' Gerard said. 'The Feckers did the same. Sher I didn't't wear any drawers after that 'till I got married and then year woman said I was a doirty fucker!

'I towelled her, de yah want me to examine yer knickers ye ould bitch?'

Siobhan reminded Gerard that Cracker was speaking.

'Ah sorry Siobhan, go on Cracker.'

'Well one day a black car arrived and I was thrown inta it. The bitches told me I was being taken to Artane. I was delighted at first because I thought I'd see me brother.'

'And did ya Cracker?" Bins asked him. Siobhan frowned and looked sternly at Bins. He looked behind him and ignored her.

'I did'n me arse Bins,' Cracker replied.

'Well if I thought those Sisters of Fuckin No Mercy were bad, they were fuckin angels in comparison to the Christian Brothers.

'I was taken to an office by two of them and the head Brother handed me a stick with leather around it, and lashes with pieces of weights in it. He told me if I didn't't behave myself I'd get this wrapped around me arse. I tell ye he frightened the shite outta me, so he did.'

Tom, Gerard. Dezzie and Bins, said the same thing in unison.

'The Leather.'

'Aye the fucking leather!' Cracker said.

'I was even put in the shoe shop making the fuckin things. The next thing I was taken to an ould fellah to get me uniform and he gave me the fright of me life. He stuck his hand up me trouser leg, he said to measure me length! Measure the fuckin length of me willie, that's what he wanted, the dirty bastard. I didn't know what was going on.

'Then I was taken to a big room with about eighty beds in it and was told this was where I was going to sleep. I remember crying and telling them "I want to see me brother, I want to see me brother!"

'Yer brother, yer brother?' the Christian Bother said to me.

'Yer brother's fuckin dead, we're the only brothers you'll ever see!'

Cracker puts his head in his hands. Ant leaned over and touched him gently on the shoulder.

'Take your fuckin hand off me,' said Cracker who looked at Ant through slit eyes threateningly.

'Nobody puts their fuckin hands on me, unless I give them permission. De yez understand?'

Ant looked embarrassed and nervous; he started to stroke his beard.

'Sorry Cracker. I didn't't mean to'

Cracker interrupted him. 'Jest don't fuckin touch me, Okay?'

Gerard intervened. 'Ah sure c'mon Cracker he was only trying to…'Cracker interrupted again. This time he shouted.

'Shut the fuck up alcho boy, ye had your say!'

The atmosphere in the room changed. Dezzie now twisted nervously in his chair and put his hands over his ears.

Siobhan, clapped her hands together gently to get everyone's attention and break the cycle of fear which was starting to grow.

'Okay everyone sit back now and take three deep breaths.'

They all did as they were asked, except Cracker; he still has his head in his hands. 'Cracker, sit up and take three deep breaths please.'

Cracker looked at Siobhan as if she was a piece of meat. Allan viewed Cracker with disgust. He was pretty sure Siobhan could hold her own but that didn't prevent the rush of adrenaline to every fibroid in his body. As big as Cracker was, he was still a street fighter. Allan, if he was pushed, could have flattened him in a second.

Siobhan looked at Cracker, softly but firmly.

'It's all right Cracker, you're safe. Breathe with me.'

Cracker seemed to come round, the expression on his face changed and he inhaled and exhaled with Siobhan. The tension in the room relaxed. Dezzie removed his hands from his ears and joined in the breathing process. When everything had calmed down. Siobhan asked Cracker if he would like to continue.

'Aye, I'm alright Siobhan, sorry lads,' said Cracker.

'Sh… Sh… Sure it's okay Cracker, yer… a g… gr… great man so ye are,' Tom said.

'Ah pay no attention to me and me big mouth Cracker,' said Gerard.

Cracker continued.

'Well it was a fuckin nightmare in there. I was always starving, we used to eat from the pig bins.'

Some of them nodded their heads in agreement; they used to do the same.

'Ah sure don't ya know.'

'Imagine. They had their own fuckin farm and used to sell everything to the community and we were all starved to death. The only time I got an egg, was at Easter! Imagine with all the fuckin chickens they had? They'd sell the fuckin eggs and we got a boiled egg for Easter! Me mammy used to give us an egg every day.'

Tom shook his head. 'I re… re… remember it well,' he said.

Cracker started talking once more.

'Sure there wasn't a day went by, without getting a fist in me face, a boot up me arse or the fuckin leather. I don't remember learning anything, though I remember a classroom with a Brother who used to have a kid standing up beside him, and he had his hand up the leg of the kid's trousers. I remember the kid crying all the time, then I didn't see the kid anymore, he just disappeared.

'Then one day McGowan knocked me down the steps, de yez remember the metal steps?'

They all nodded in agreement.

'I do so, I was kicked up them, and thrown down them enough shagging times!' said Bins, again as he looked behind him.

'Well, the bastard,' Cracker said, 'shoved me down the fuckin steps, for no reason. Then he picked me up by me locks, dragged me inta the office and laid inta me with the leather.

'I remember he was foaming white stuff from his mouth and I couldn't understand a word he was saying. I just kept screaming at him to stop; shouting I was sorry, sorry and I wouldn't do it again. Though for the fuck of me I didn't know what I'd done.'

Dezzie took a sip of water; Siobhan asked them all to do the same.

'I spent a week in the sick-room after that, lying on my stomach 'cause the backs of me legs were cut ta ribbons, I still have the scars.'

Cracker stood up, turned his back to them, pulled up the legs of his sweat pant up to his knees and showed them purple, striped scars.

They all looked at them and shook their heads.

'Shaggin feckers,' said Bins.

'Bastards,' said Gerard.

Ant murmured something that sounded like the words Jesus Christ under his breath.

'Evil, that's what they were. Devils.' Everyone looked at Dezzie as it was the first time he had spoken.

Cracker sat down.

'Then when I was around 13 a few of us were taken to a place for a holiday. I can't remember where it was. It was summer and there was a forest and a beach and a big old half empty house with loads of rooms.

McGowan was there with three other brothers. One of them was old fat Brother Michael. Duz any of ye remember him?'

'Y... y... yeah, I rem... rem... remember him,' Tom said, 'sh... sure... he was the one who gave out the clothes, and fe... felt you up!'

'That's the one, so he was there then when you were there?'

'He was that,' replied Tom, momentarily losing his stutter.

'Well the first time we went down to the strand,' Cracker said, 'he brought the swimming togs and made all of us strip off to try them on; and he was having a feel of all of us, pretending the togs were too big or too small. The dirty fucker.

'I wouldn't't let him touch me and McGowan gave me a clip, which knocked me sideways and I could hear ringing in me ear. I don't know what happened to me but, I picked up a rock and threw it at him, it missed him but caught one of the boys on the leg and cut his leg.

'McGowan got hold of me by the ears and dragged me back to the house. There was a lay-man working there and he helped McGowan get hold of me. They dragged me inta the kitchen and started boxing me around the place. Then they bent me over the table'

Cracker started to sweat; he put his hands up to his face. He stopped speaking and started breathing deeply, his voice changed to a whimper.

'That lay fellah held me over the table and McGowan ripped the togs off me, and then, and then, and then, the fucker…'

Cracker stopped speaking, the tears spilled over his face.

'Well what he did to me destroyed me. From that day I never felt like a man. No matter what I did or how hard I tried to be like what I thought was a man, it didn't work. It was like I couldn't feel, like as if I was one big blank thing. I'd look at those comic books with big strong men in them and try to be like that but no matter how big or how strong I became I couldn't feel.'

There was total silence in the room. The men were not shocked, it was as if a candle had been snuffed out and they we were sitting in the dark with their own dark memories. They had no words of comfort which would express how they felt. Ant went to put his hand on Cracker's shoulder and froze, he put his hand down.

'It's all right Cracker, you're safe here, it's alright.'

Cracker pulled himself together.

'Well after that, the bastard had me where he wanted me, I was that terrified. He only had to point at me and I followed him like a fuckin lamb. Usually down to the boiler room. I used to pray every night for God to take me, I used to cry when I woke up every morning, mind you I wasn't the only one crying in that dormitory. The poor buggers who woke up and realized they had wet their beds would be crying and shivering with fright. Then one night I lost the run of meself. I took a knife from the kitchen and yer man was in the room next to the dormitory. I went in and held the knife at his bollix and told him if he ever touched me again, I'd cut him ta pieces, and by God I meant it. Well, he never did touch me again, he never as much as looked at me.'

Cracker looked around at all of them.

'I've followed that bastard all me life. He was sent out to the Missions for a while. Christ knows what he did to those poor black bastards!

I even bumped into him one day on the street. I did it on the purpose like, and he didn't even recognize me! Can ya imagine, he did that ta me and he didn't't even recognize me?

'Oh I know where he is alright. He's in a small house, with three other retired bastards at the back of Glasnevin graveyard. Every night before he goes to bed, no matter what the weather, he takes a walk around the graveyard, sits on a bench and smokes his pipe.'

Crackers voice became quiet, his eyes like slits.

'He fuckin destroyed me life, and there he sits like a fuckin old grandfather smoking his fuckin pipe every night!'

He shook his head, as if he was waking up from a bad dream.

'Did ya ever find yer brother Cracker?' asked Bins, as he looked behind him.

'I did. Me father died a year after I got out of Artane and I met him then. He'd been in Daingean, the fuckin Alcatraz of Ireland. God knows what happened to him in there. Sure we didn't have anything in common like. He took after me father and went on the piss, nearly fell into me father's grave so he did at the funeral. A year later he threw himself off a bridge in England and that was the end of him. I didn't even go to the funeral; sure it was like he was a stranger to me.'

'And wh... wh... what about your sis... sister Cracker?' Tom asked.

'I never saw her again. To this day I don't know what happened her. I heard that me father went on the piss after we were taken, and the parish priest made sure that she was taken away as well, but I've never been able to find her. I tried a year ago, through that new office with the freedom of information thing, but still nothing.

'I lived with the hate of what they did to me for years. I went to England, lied about me age and enlisted in the army. Sure I was a mad fucker and got thrown out after a bit of training. I couldn't't take orders ye see, I was what they called out-of-control.

'Then I met a couple of other Irish fellas and we ended up joining a private army and going to the Congo.'

'You mean you became a mercenary Cracker?' asked Ant.

'What's that, is it like a missionary?' asked Bins.

'No Bins it isn't. It is like a private army where they get well paid. They go into any country and fight.'

'I did,' said Cracker, 'and what's more I loved every fuckin minute of it. It was like the gun was growing out of me hand, it became part of me. Pointing it was like pointing me finger, pulling the trigger was like scratching an itch. The only thing I never shot were children.'

'Does that mean you shot women?' Bins asked.

'I did so, sher you'd never know which side they were on anyways! I hated everyone, pulling that trigger was the only thing that gave me head some peace.

'I hated women as much as I hated the men. I blamed me mother for dying on me, and those fuckin Sisters of No Mercy for the bitches they were. How could ye respect a woman after them lot? I'd no more trust a woman then fly to the fuckin moon.

'Well I travelled around a bit, though I keep that to meself, it's my business, and then I came back to Ireland.

'I thought I was alright until this fuckin abuse thing came up on the news and changed everything. It stirred my head up and made me think too much. I was never any good at holding my temper but I became worse and worse. To tell you the truth I became so angry I started to prowl the streets at night just looking for someone to tear the head off him.

'Then me son was born and I knew I had to change.'

'Yes,' said Ant, 'children change all of us in some way, and the last thing we want is for the children to suffer the way we did, no one deserves that.'

They all nodded their heads in agreement.

'I had to stop using me fists and start using me head.'

'Siobhan encouraged me to go back to school because I could hardly read, and I did. I went to an English class. I felt like a real eejit at first but sher everyone was in the same boat.

'Then I started writing me poetry. As I got into me relaxation, breathing and the hypnosis, me anger became less, it's still there mind, but like I've more control on it, and me poetry got better.

'Poetry. I thought that stuff was only for poofs.'

Siobhan interrupted him before he could finish the word.

'Shh, be quiet Bins.'

'It was a great way to get me feelings out. I had some published and won a few prizes, so I know I'm not as thick as I thought I was.

'It was when I started coming to Siobhan I realized how badly I'd been damaged as a child, and I've worked hard the last two years with her. I know I'm not normal but I'm a hell of a lot nearer normal than I was.

'There again, I'm a hell of a lot more normal then those fuckers who did what they did to me. Sher I was only a child, only a little kid.

'They shoulda closed them places down years ago, they were nothing more than torture chambers for kids and breeding grounds for pedophiles and perverts.'

'Yer right there, Cracker. They should all be collected up and shot, so they should. Sher they're still picking up the criminals from the last war, the ones that put all them people in the gas chambers. They should be doing the shaggin same here.'

Bins looked at Cracker and then behind himself twice. 'I say they should all be hanged and then shot!'

Ant stroked his beard.

'Nothing changes in this country,' he said. 'State protects the church, church protects the State. When was it any different?

'You know when you think of it, all those institutions were there just for the religious to make money, and they made a fortune from them.'

'How s... so Ant, Wha... What de ya mean Ant?' Tom asked.

'Well if you look at it this way Tom, Every time a judge sent a child to one of these hell- holes, who got paid?'

'The shaggin religious, that's who.' said Bins.

'Yes,' answered Ant. 'They got paid a lot of money for those days, considering they spent a pittance on each child. As you said Cracker, you were starving, all of you were starving. All of you had to eat out of the pig bins, or if you were lucky you worked on the farm and could steal a carrot and even eat it with the dirt on it.'

Ant stroke his goatee beard and lowered his eyes, he wondered if he had said too much, maybe he should keep his opinions to himself as he usually did.

'Yer r… right Ant. Many's the t… time I did that, a… and m… many's the time I got k… kicked to t… the ground for getting c… caught!' said Tom.

'Sure if the State gave the money to the child's family, instead of to the Holy Joe's, none of this would have happened,' Ant explained.

'And not one of those institutions paid any tax on their income because they were classed as Charitable Institutions!'

'Charitable Institutions me shaggin arse,' Bins interrupted.

'Sure it's a shaggin disgrace. I never looked at it like dat before.'

'Neither did I?' said Gerard.

'Charitable me hole!' Cracker said. He now turned his attention towards Dezzie. He looked at him twice.

Dezzie avoided eye-contact, and started brushing imaginary fluff from his trousers.

'Hey, ye. I'm speaking to ye. What about ye? Ye've said nothing yet,' said Cracker.

Dezzie didn't respond.

'For fucks sake. Are ye deaf as well as dumb?' Siobhan looked at Cracker as she interjected.

'Cracker, why are you shouting at Dezzie?'

'I'm not shouting, I'm asking him a question,' he shouted.

'You are raising your voice and we call that shouting!'

'Why are you shouting at Dezzie?'

'Well. We are meant to be a Group.' To emphasise the point, he placed an index finger to each temple. 'So why is he standing outside the group?'

'May be,' responded Siobhan, 'that is where Dezzie feels more comfortable right now. 'What makes you feel uncomfortable with that?'

'Ah fer fuck's sake Siobhan, would ye get a grip. Either yer in the group and talking, or outta the group with yer fuckin gob shut.'

'As long as Dezzie is sitting quietly listening, then he's participating. OK? Cracker?' said Siobhan.

Gerard intervened.

'For feck's sake Cracker, yr not the feckin Lone Ranger here. Stop trying ta bully the man.'

Cracker rose from his chair and glared at Gerard.

'Who are ye calling a fuckin bully? Ye skinny fuckin Casius Clay ye.'

Gerard rose slowly from his seat.

Chapter 9

ALLAN WENT into high alert; he hated the language they were using in front of Siobhan. He felt like picking her up in his arms and taking her out of the building. He wondered to himself if a Ferrari was in any way similar to a white horse. Under the circumstances his Harley Davidson might be more appropriate.

He had no idea Siobhan worked with men as aggressive as they were. How she had the strength to hold them back and keep some form of control, was beyond him.

Siobhan lowered her voice. She looked at the two sparring partners. Cracker was using his bullying tactics to disarm Gerard, who was now going to use his body as a buffer to safeguard Siobhan from any abuse.

'That's enough you two. Sit down and cut the crap out of your body language Cracker. Mouthing off, threatening language and behaviour it doesn't belong in this room. Stop acting and start listening and feeling.'

Cracker sat back in his chair, stiff with tension and still glaring at Gerard who ignored him. There was silence in the room, an uncomfortable silence.

'Okay gentlemen; let's take a few minutes out to relax. Tom would you mind opening the windows for a minute please and let the tension out of this room?'

Tom was delighted to be able to do something for Siobhan. He hated the shouting. Loud voices made him nervous. Aggressive behavior terrified him. Siobhan smiled at him when he looked over at her, reassuring him everything was under control.

Slightly raising her diamond pendant with her forefinger she asked them all to close their eyes.

'I'd like you all to take three deep breaths and exhale out as if you are blowing through a straw. You all know how to do it. Relax and imagine you are in your safe place.'

Siobhan had taught all of them how to choose their safe place, a place where they were calm and at peace.

The room became more tranquil; their breathing reached the same pace. Siobhan relaxed knowing they were all safe.

Allan closed his eyes but he didn't need a safe place, unless he had to whisk Siobhan away from what he termed as 'the madness!'

Five minutes passed and they heard Siobhan's voice in the distance.

'I'd like you all to open your eyes, in your own time,' she said.

'Three, two, one. You are safe, open your eyes.'

They opened their eyes, looked at each other and smiled or nodded. The room was no longer a battle ground. It had returned to the peaceful haven it was.

'Dezzie,' Siobhan said, 'would you mind closing the windows for me please?'

Dezzie got up from his chair, with a slight mincing step he walked to the windows and closed them. On his way back to his chair he smiled at Cracker.

Cracker returned the smile.

Observing the lack of animosity from Cracker and the lack of fear from Dezzie, Allan was astonished.

'What the hell was that all about?' he thought. 'How the hell did that happen?'

'How do you feel Dezzie?' Siobhan asked.

'I'm fine thanks Siobhan.'

'Is there anything you would like to say Dezzie?'

'Well I don't know what to say really Siobhan. I suppose what Gerard and Cracker said has had a profound effect on me, it kind of leaves me speechless. The pain of your experiences,' he looked first at Gerard, then Cracker, 'is unbelievable. I don't know how you survived so much pain.'

'May I interrupt you please Dezzie?'

Siobhan looked at all of them, as if she was skimming the room with her eyes.

'As I said in the beginning. There is no scale to measure pain in this room. Unbearable has a different meaning for all of you.

'What I sense at the moment is, you are all starting to bond with each other and understand the similarities and differences you all share.

'I'd like to ask each of you, to give me one word to describe what you are feeling right now.'

Siobhan reached for a small pad and pen, preparing to start writing down their answers.

She gave them a few minutes to get their thoughts in order.

'Tom, just one word please?'

'Freedom.'

'Gerard?'

Respect and…' Siobhan gently interrupts, 'just one word please Gerard.'

'Respect.'

'Ant?'

'Incredible.'

'Bins?'

'Emotion.'

'Cracker?

'Numb.'

'Dezzie?

'Disgraceful.'

'Allan?'

'Strangers.'

Siobhan wrote on her pad, stopped and frowned.

'Thank you very much. Now this is quite incredible! Do you know if you take the first letter of each word you have given me, it spells the word friends.'

The men all looked at each other in amazement.

'That's shaggin creepy,' said Bins, as he glanced over his shoulder.

'Not really,' Ant said, stroking his beard, 'because that's what I feel. I feel as if I am surrounded by really dear friends.'

'Me tt… too,' said Tom.

'I'm a loner,' Cracker mumbled, 'I don't really know what it's like to have friends, but if it feels like this, then I like the feeling.'

'I feel we are very special people,' Gerard added.

'I'm always frightened of people, especially people I've just met, but I feel safe here with all of you,' Dezzie said.

Allan felt he was the fly in the ointment and decided to be diplomatic.

'One can never have too many friends.'

'It was difficult to have friends in the institutions wasn't it?' Siobhan asked.

They all nodded their heads affirming the truth of this statement.

'Would anyone like to talk about that?' Siobhan asked.

Cracker was the first to respond. 'I had one once. His name was Whippet. He was small and as fast as a fuckin whippet. Them bastard brothers could never catch him, he was that fast. We were great mates he covered for me, and I covered for him. He'd steal the jam and I'd steal the bread. We'd steal every piece of bread we could get our hands on.

'Sometimes we'd take the bread out to the pig bins and try to find an ould piece of meat to make a sandwich, any old thing we could find. Once it was the sole of an old shoe! Sure we didn't't care.

'One day they caught us and dragged us up to McGowan's room. I'll never forget it. They made us eat the bread and kept clattering us on the head trying to force us to eat the sole of the shoe. They were laughing at us and calling us names. They were tearing bits off the sole of the shoe and ramming it in our gobs. Then they started laying into us with their fists and the leather. I was crying but nothing wud make Whippet cry, nothing!'

'McGowan said "let's shake the food out of the little bastard." They tied his hands behind his back and tied his legs together, then they threw him out of the window head first holding onto his ankles. He screamed and choked and vomited. Then there was a mighty crack and I think one of his legs got broke, unless it was the sound of his head against the wall, I don't know. I shite me self with the fright. Them bastards were all laughing and I was crying because I knew they'd do the fuckin same to me self.

'When they pulled Whippet back in through the window his face was grey and his tongue was hanging out funny.'

Cracker paused, as if he was trying to remember something.

'He didn't' move, not even a twitch. They slapped him on the back and on the face but he still didn't move. Then they wrapped him in a sheet and carried him away. McGowan gave me a boot up the arse and told me not to open me mouth or I'd get the same. I never saw Whippet again.'

Tears ran down Cracker's cheeks. Ant offered him the box of tissues.

'Tanks Ant,' he said.

'Would you like to take a walk outside Cracker?'

'Ah, no, sure I'm alright Siobhan. Let's get on with it.'

'Sher they'd accuse you of scamping or fiddling wid each other, if you had a friend,' Bins said.

'Then they'd watch you to see if you had a special friend, and they'd shaggin get one of yez inta the office and tell yr friend said this about yez, and they'd tell yez something like a lie yer man was meant to'uve told on yez.'

'Then ye'd get a beating because of the lie and you'd shagging go outta there and beat the shite outta your friend.

And sure ya learned not ta trust anyone, dats why ya never had a shaggin friend.'

'Sh… sh… Sher I c… couldn't trust m… me own sh… sh… shadow! Sh… sh… sher… if I saw m me own sh… shadow b… behind me I'd die of fright, I'd think I was be being f… follered,' Tom said.

Gerard started to speak, his fake teeth moving slightly out of place, correcting them with his thumb he didn't notice the slight dribble down his chin.

'We couldn't't trust each other, therefore we were isolated, and they could pick us off like flies. We couldn't't trust and we grew into men that couldn't trust. I've never been able to trust anyone but you Siobhan. It's called conquer and provide so it is…that was the message we got.'

Bins looked behind him and, 'yer right there Ger, they succeeded dividing us all. There was no one we could talk to but ourselves and I'm still doing that, the only trouble is I'm answering myself now!'

They all nodded and sat quietly. Siobhan looked over at Dezzie and smiled at him, he returned the smile and asked her quietly, 'will I speak now Siobhan?'

'If you feel comfortable Dezzie go ahead, if you have to stop don't worry and don't force yourself.'

'Well I think I can manage it Siobhan.'

Dezzie looked around the room and took a deep breath.

'I don't know that much about myself, a lot of my memories have gone because I had a procedure, and sometimes I'm not sure if a memory is real or not.

'A lot of what I know is what Siobhan researched for me through the Freedom of Information Act. My mother was a junkie. She prostituted herself to get her fixes.

'I was born a junkie, she'd taken that much gear, it went into me when I was in her womb, so when I was born I was already a heroin addict. They wouldn't' let her have me, said I was at risk!

'In the light of what happened to me afterwards, I was more at risk being a Ward of the State, than with her! I was born in Offaly and taken to the county home. I heard it took five months to clean my system out of the heroin and shit she used to take.

'I don't remember much until I was about three. There was a lovely girl there, now she would only have been about twelve herself, and she looked after me like I was her doll.

Then I think I was about six when I was fostered out to the Wicked Witch of the West. Did you ever see that film Somewhere Over the Rainbow with Judy Garland?'

'Ah God I loved that film, must ave seen it a thousand times,' said Gerard.

He started mimicking Garland singing. Throwing a left and right pretend plait over each shoulder. Bins Laughed and looked behind him. Ant frowned, stroked his beard and looked at Siobhan.

Cracker shouted threateningly across to Gerard.

'Would ye ever sit down ye fuckin eejit two left feet man and let the man talk.'

'Who the feck are you calling a two left feet man, when you don't even know a man from a woman? Who da ya think you are? The Sundance Kid?'

Cracker got out of his chair and took a step towards Gerard, who got out of his chair and stared tap dancing towards the door.

'Cracker sit down,' Siobhan told him. Cracker looked at her menacingly.

'Cracker please sit down!'

Siobhan turned to Gerard.

'Everyone listened to your story with respect, we would all appreciate it if you did the same.'

'Ah sorry Siobhan, sorry lads, I just thought I'd lighten it up a bit!'

No one laughed. Gerard looked embarrassed.

'Fuckin Eejit,' mumbled Cracker.

Siobhan now looked at Dezzie.

'Sorry about the interruption Dezzie would you like to continue?'

'It's okay Siobhan, they were just letting off a bit of steam. Anyway she looked just like her, except for the hait, I can't even bear to say her name.'

Dezzie trembled slightly, then continued.

'She was well paid by the State to nearly kill me. Not only me, her old father was beaten to a pulp half the time. If it wasn't me, it was him she was kicking around the place.

'She was out of her skull. She had a farm miles away from anywhere, but her husband was in the army and hardly ever there.

'I had a lovely room with a few toys in it, but I was only allowed in that room if her husband was there or the odd time when the Social Services came to check on me. Sure they were useless, most of the time they didn't't even see me, they'd just give me a wave when I was out in the yard.

She was all sweetness and light with them, but she hated me.'

'That's terrible,' said Tom. He looked at Bins and said, 'Isn't that terrible Bins?'

Looking behind himself Bins replied, 'Ah sure don't ya know?'

Dezzie continued. 'She would skin the legs off me with a piece of knotted rope, or a wire hanger. She beat me in places where it wouldn't' show, like me back, arse and the top of my legs.'

'Jesus Christ!' said Ant, stroking his beard.

'Yes. Then when they were bleeding, she'd clatter the face off me if the blood went on the floor. She'd give me a rag and throw me on the floor. Push me down with her foot on my back and keep me there 'till I'd cleaned off every drop.

'Sometimes the blood would go on my pajamas', she'd call me a dirty bastard and make me stand on a stool over the sink and scrub my pajamas. While I was doing that the blood from my legs would drip on the floor again, and she'd throw me on the floor and make me mop it up again.'

Dezzie paused and ran his fingers through his hair, then tied the band around his pony tail a little tighter.

'There was a cupboard in the hall, not much bigger than myself. It had an old bit of carpet in it and a smelly cushion. That's where she used to make me sleep. In the summer it was boiling hot, in the winter it was freezing.

'It was the one place I felt safe because when she threw me in there she would be exhausted, I knew she wouldn't have the energy to start on me again until the next day. The only friend I had was a cow, an old heffer. I used to talk to that cow as if he was a boy like myself.'

Ant wrapped his arms around himself and started to gently rock to and fro.

'Then when I started going to school I was frightened of everyone but kind of happy because the teachers were nice to me.

'I think it must have been one of them that called the social, because I was taken away and put in the county home again and then sent to St Josephs. I'll never forget the day I was put in there.

'We got to a big building and I remember it was pouring with rain and I was very scared because it reminded me of a story I heard about a haunted castle.

'I was told this was Letterfrack and it was where I was going to stay. There were terrible smells and to this day I smell them when I go into places like old hospitals.'

Dezzie started to sweat and shake, which prompted Bins to interrupt.

'Ah now, don't you know? Feckin Letterfrack.'

'Well I worked in the kitchen, so it wasn't all bad.'

Bins interrupted Dezzie again. 'Well you must have been a pretty boy then, because only the good looking kids worked in the kitchen.'

'I remember one day being lined up with the other kids, girls and boys and they shaved all my hair off. Then they painted all my body with white stuff that smelled and stung the life out of me. I got a slap across the face because I was crying and hopping around the bathroom. I think they did this because there was some kinda disease going around'.

Siobhan could see that Dezzie was sweating more, she wanted to give him the opportunity to withdraw.

'It's okay Dezzie if you want to stop now.'

'No, Siobhan, I'll just have a sup of water please.'

Ant handed him a glass of water, with trembling hands. Dezzie took a sip.

Tom looked at Gerard, and Gerard returned the look with a sympathetic shrug. Siobhan had never heard Dezzie speak so much without it being practically sucked out of him. She was delighted he felt safe and comfortable enough to keep going.

Dezzie sighed and continued.

'There isn't't much I remember about Letterfrack. Siobhan says I still suffer from dissociation, which means I disassociate myself from most of the bad things that happened to me. Also I had electric shocks to my brain a few years ago for depression. That obliterated a lot of my memories thank God. The least memories I have the better I am.'

'What's that word mean?' Bins asked.

Ant, who was losing patience with all the interruptions from Bins, asked him what he was talking about.

'Obliate or something,' Bins said and looked behind him.

'It means wiped out or got rid of his memories,' Ant replied.

Dezzie now continued. 'When things really get bad for me I hide in my safe place. My safe place is the cupboard or the wardrobe. When I do sleep in a bed it has to be a very small bed, like a child's bed. I have special blankets. I've had them for years. I don't like them washed because they lose their safe smell. The cupboard is better, I can melt into the wood; it's my safe place.'

The men looked uncomfortable, quickly glancing at each other and at Siobhan.

Bins looked up at the ceiling. 'Sher that's all right Dezzie, my shaggin safe place is standing on a chair.'

'And my safe place is sitting on the feckin toilet reading feckin Playboy,' said Gerard. 'It's the only place yer woman can't get inta.' Siobhan gave Gerard a warning look and he gave a gesture of zipping up his lips.

Dezzie didn't seem to hear Gerard's remark, he was staring into space.

'There was a man that ran the farm there; he did bad things to me, things that hurt. I used to try to make myself invisible; I used to pretend no one could see me.

'One summer that man with the red hair was there. He did a bad thing to me, like what he did to you Cracker. There was a lot of blood and he used to make me clean it up. If I cried he'd lick me on the shins with his big boot, my shins were always black and blue.

'One day he knocked my front teeth out because I wouldn't't let him put his, you know, his, his, his thing in my mouth. There was a lot of blood then. I had to be taken to the nurse and he told her I'd fallen and knocked my teeth out. After that they said I was a trouble-maker and a liar, they took me out of the kitchen.

'They sent me out to cut the turf every day. It didn't't matter what the weather, hot or freezing cold. I had to stand for hours with the freezing water going over the top of my boots, and the boots rubbing my legs till they were red raw. I was very slow cutting the turf and that farm man used to knock me over, call me names and hit me with the spade.

'I don't think there was a day when I didn't cry, I was always frightened. I wanted to run away but I didn't't know which way to run because it was miles away from anywhere.

The food was terrible but I never got very much because the boys at my table would take mine.

'I got a boiled egg for Easter as well. Sometimes if important people were visiting we'd get jam and extra things. I used to wet the bed and that was the worst thing to do. Any of us who wet the bed were beaten senseless and they made us wrap the sheets around our head and walk around the dormitory for hours. At night I couldn't sleep for some of the boys crying. I was too terrified to cry. I still find it difficult to cry but I have started to feel things that I never felt before.

'When I first came to see Siobhan and she asked me "how do you feel?" I didn't know what she was talking about because I couldn't feel anything it was like being numb all over. We've done a lot of work around that and I know now how to feel sad, but it is difficult for me to know how to feel happy. I was put on a train to Dublin with five shillings in my pocket when I was fifteen and that was that.

I got a job in a bakers and the owner let me sleep on the floor near the ovens. In two months, I saved up the money to catch the boat train to London.

'I didn't know anyone, I slept in shop doorways, under bridges and anywhere I could get out of the rain. I met other lads like myself or runaways and they taught me how to find food and beg. Then I became a rent boy.'

The men looked at each other.

Gerard asked what that was.

'Was it collecting the rents for someone, like the feckin Mafia, like breaking people's legs if they didn't pay ya?'

Cracker looked shocked. 'Yer a dirty fucker so ya are!'

'What, what did he say?' asked Gerard. 'What's the matter with you now lone ranger?'

Cracker pointed his finger threateningly at Gerard.

'Will ye stop fucking calling me Lone Ranger yer fuckin skinny boxer ye? He was fuckin taking it up the arse, for fuckin money so he was!'

Bins looked at Cracker. 'Well I bet you shaggin took it up the arse in the Joy, but you were too shaggin ugly to get paid for it.'

'Ah lads. Will youse h... h... have a bit of res... respect now and let Dezzie f... finish his st... sto... story. Sh... Shure we're n not here t... t... tugh... judge any wo... one!' stuttered Tom.

Siobhan now intervened.

'You have all learned how to be non-judgmental so put it into practice. Cracker get hold of yourself now please. Show a bit of respect as Tom said.'

'Maybe that's his fuckin trouble; he hasn't anything ta get holed of,' remarked Gerard.

Cracker started to rise from his chair.

'I' told yeee…'

Siobhan interrupted.

'Sit down in the fucking chair Cracker, and cut the threatening behavior, you don't have to prove you're a big man in this room!'

Cracker sat down, still staring at Gerard, who ignored him.

Siobhan looked at Dezzie.

'Go on Dezzie please. I want the rest of you to be quiet, and stop personalizing arguments and thoughts.'

Allan, smiled to himself thinking, she actually said the F word. Maybe she isn't the Ice Maiden after all. I suppose sometimes it isn't enough to walk in someone's shoes you have to use their language as well he mused to himself.

Siobhan glanced at Allan, he felt she was challenging him in some way, or, maybe she could read his thoughts.

Dezzie now continued. 'Well, then I met a man who took me in, he was a nice old man and he was very good to me.'

'Ah well that's n… nice. Everyone should have s someone, th… that's me motto,' Tom said.

'He sent me to school to learn hairdressing. I wasn't much good at it but at least I could get a job. Eventually

I was offered a job on an American cruise ship. I loved that, did it for about fifteen years, then I met the love of my life.'

Cracker looked up at the ceiling.

'Fer f……'

Siobhan gave him a warning look. He shut his mouth.

'We were very happy. Well I was very happy.

He was different to me. He was an actor, all his family were actors. I suppose you could say he was born with a silver spoon in his mouth.

Bins interjected. 'Jayzus the only thing tha was in my mouth when I was born was me ma's ould tit, so it was.'

'Anyway he had a house in Weybridge and another one in Waterford. His parents had houses in the South of France and Switzerland. We spent a lot of time here. Then he got sick and we stayed here most of the time, it was more private then England.

'I didn't tell him any of my background, I told him my parents were dead and I was brought up by an old aunt who died. Anyway he died last year with AIDS and I'm waiting to die now, I'm HIV positive.'

Cracker jumped out of his chair on hearing this.

'Ah fer fucks sake, that's it. I'm outta here, I'm not breathing in the same fuckin air as him!'

'As you like Cracker.' Siobhan said.

Cracker looked surprised, as if he expected her to prevent him from leaving.

Siobhan pointed at the door.

'The doors over there.'

'Right so,' he said and started walking towards the door. He left. The room was quiet. None of them had expected Siobhan to react as she had.

Bins jumped up.

'The shaggin arsehole, I'll go and shaggin sort him out Siobhan.'

From outside there was a lot of shouting, inside the men listened quietly. They could hear Bins remonstrating.

'Hey big man, how shaggin big are you te be shaggin frightened of a shaggin virus?'

'Ugh?' grunted Cracker.

'Well me own son has the shaggin thing, he gorrit through a shaggin needle,' Bins shouted.

'What was he fuckin doin? Cracker shouted back. 'Takin up the hem of his skirt?'

'Listen big man, have a look at me shaggin rings. Have a look will ya?' Bins shouts.

'What the fuck are them things?' Cracker said.

'Shaggin solid steel so they shaggin are, enough to rip yer shaggin head off. And if yer don't get in there and shaggin apologise to Siobhan, yer shaggin head's gonna be up in that shaggin tree. De ya get me?'

There was silence. The men in the room looked at each other. Allan was secretly hoping Cracker would just leave, or Bins would rip his head off.

'Ah shurr well, I suppose I went a bit over the top,' Cracker said. 'I'll go back in, but I'm not fuckin sitting next to that fuckin nancy boy.'

Cracker came back into the room followed by Bins.

'Sorry Siobhan, sure ye know how I am when I lose the head. Sorry Dezzie, I gotta bit of a fright. I'm scared of sickness.'

Dezzie accepted Cracker's apology.

'Every one's scared of AIDS Cracker, it's Okay. Welcome back Cracker,' said Siobhan.

Cracker Squeezed himself between Gerard and Tom on the settee. Gerard got up, walked over to Cracker's chair, sat down next to Dezzie and put his arm around his shoulder.

'Sure there's plenty of fuckin life in yer yet lad. They have great cures for this thing now and there's always loads of those alternating therapies,' Gerard said, giving Dezzie's shoulder a squeeze.

'I don't want a cure, I just want to die. I want to be near him.'

'Sure there's no guarantee if ya die,' said Gerard, 'that y'ell be near him lad. Life is for the living, what yer need is a nice girl ta look after ya.'

'I'm gay Gerard!'

'Sure, I'm gay nearly every day as well Dezzie. You can't be unhappy all the time now, can ya?'

The men looked at each other and smiled, except for Cracker who rolled his eyes to heaven. Siobhan nodded, showing her approval of Gerard's gentleness with Dezzie.

Dezzie nodded his head and looked down rubbing his hands together.

'I don't know, I just don't know half the time, what I'm thinking or what I'm doing.'

'Sure it's a shagging good holiday ya need,' said Bins looking behind him.

'A shaggin foreign place out of this shaggin country, that's what ya need Dezzie me lad!'

'My mother took me to Paris six months ago, but all I did was cry because I remembered when he took me there. I cried up the Eiffel Tower and down the Seine, I even cried on the Left Bank.'

Cracker interjected once again.

'I thought ye told us your fucking mother was dead!'

'No. I didn't. I said she was a junkie!

'She found me a year ago. She went through that new Freedom of Information Act thing and they got in touch with me and I met her.

'She's clean now and a lovely woman, real motherly she is.

'She never had any more children and she always wanted to make it up to me what she did. She's married to an ould fellah but he's very nice to me. I live in their bungalow in Santry. It's nice; I have my own room with a television and everything.

'Jim, that's her husband, even put a little shower and toilet in the room for me like an en-suite, it's even got a bidet in it,' said Dezzie.

'I thought a Bidet was a shagging piece of bread, what would ya be doin with a piece of bread in the bathroom?' said Bins, who looked behind him.

'Bins, a bidet is like a little toilet you sit on, you press a button and the water comes up and showers your bum,' said Ant.

'Ah get away outta that which ya fer God's sake, pull the other one Sher, what would ya want to shagging shower your bum for. What about the shaggin rest of ya?'

'Ah fer fucks sake,' said Cracker. 'This is getting ridicerliss!'

'It might be fuckin ridicerliss to you Lone Ranger, but maybe Dezzie likes to shower his arse,' Gerard said.

'Oh, I bet he fuckin does, say no more, say no more!' replied Cracker.

'Well,' said Gerard. 'I tell ya Dezzi lad, whenever ya want to go anywhere, just say the word. I'll give ya me number and anytime ya want to go out, not for a pint mind you, but anything else, I'm yer man, just give me a tinkle and I'll be which ya.'

'Thanks Gerard.'

'No thanks required.'

There was a warmth in the room. Camaraderie seems to have replaced the antagonism. The miracle of healing starts with sharing Siobhan believed. These men had started to share, not only their personal pain but each other's pain.

Very often during the therapeutic process there was a stage which was self-centered. Each client was focused on themselves. Clients had to go through this stage as a form of self-protection. Sometime or another they had to learn to put themselves first. She thought, when we give all of our-self away, there is nothing to share. These men had everything taken away from them when they were just children. How could they grow, as a human beings, if they hadn't learned integrity, pride and self-value. It simply wasn't possible.

'Thank you Dezzie for sharing your life with us. How are you feeling now?'

'Well I can feel that I have a lot of friends Siobhan, and with your help as well, I suppose I might have bit of hope.'

Siobhan smiled at him and nodded her head in agreement. He now had what he needed, Gerard the professional mentor, they'll be good for each other.

Ant stroked his beard and looked around the room.

'If it's okay with you all, I'd like to tell my story.'

They all looked at him eagerly. They were not alone anymore; they had friends who they could talk to without feeling the shame. Friends that accepted them for whom they were. Friends without any expectations. Why had they had to spend most of their lives hiding? They wondered.

'First of all,' Ant said, 'I want to tell you that my story is not like yours and I feel really honored to be here with you all this evening.

'After I tell you my story I am prepared to leave the Group if that is what you all wish!'

The men were confused; they looked at each other and at Siobhan questioningly.

'I was born in Carlow. There were four of us, all boys and I was the eldest. My father was killed by a car one night swaying down the lane on his way back from the pub. I was seven at the time. The driver said "Daddy just walked in front of his car." He couldn't avoid him. Sure he always swayed himself back from the pub anyway, so I suppose it would have happened soon or later.

'Anyway between the jigs and the reels I was sent to my grandfather's farm, my mother's father, to help him and because I'd be one less mouth for my mother to feed.

'My mother was a hard woman, she didn't really like kids and she hated the sight of me. There wasn't a day went by without her giving me a slap with the back of hairbrush, and when she broke a few of them she'd hit me with the poker.

'I can tell you, the day I was packed off to my grandfather I was delighted. Little did I know then, that my whole life would change. My childhood would be terminated. I would have to live with the appalling memories of those years, playing over and over in my head, until the day I walked in here and met Siobhan.

'I suppose all of us lived with the shame of what happened to us, even though we recognize that the legacy is not our shame, it is theirs! They were the adults, we were the children,' said Ant, who paused before he stroked his beard.

'We somehow got to believe that it was our fault; it was because we were bad and no one could love us. That's why I never spoke about it, I felt dirty and when I grew up I felt less than a man.'

The men nodded their heads in agreement.

'In fact I didn't know what it was to be a man.

'I felt nothing; as if I didn't' belong to the human race and as if I was always standing outside a circle looking in.

'When I was about twenty I started cutting myself. First of all it was my stomach and every time I did it, it made me feel better, like somehow I was cleansed and the bad was coming out of me. Then I'd cut my arms.'

He pulled up his sleeves and showed them the scars on his upper arms, he had inflicted on himself. Then it got worse. He stroked his beard once more and looked at the floor.

'I started cutting my penis. That made me feel even better. One day I cut it so deep it wouldn't stop bleeding and I had to call an ambulance.

'I was taken to the hospital and they stitched it up. They wouldn't let me go home until a psychiatrist had seen me. He was as thick as two planks and asked me how I did it? I told him I was practicing shaving and the razor slipped!'

'Jesus Ant,' Gerard said. 'Were you not using a feckin safety razor or what?'

'No Gerard I was using an ordinary razor blade!'

'Shaggin hell, it's a wunder ya didn't cut your shaggin prick off!' said Bins, his hands between his legs, subconsciously protecting himself.

'Ah wwwell… Ant, I know the the.. d… damage th… them things ca can do. God Help y ya,' said Tom.

Ant continued telling the story.

'They discharged me and that was that. I tell you I got such a terrible fright, I stopped cutting myself.'

Siobhan spoke quietly.

'Ant, why don't you tell us what happened to you, when you went to live with your granda?'

'Yes, I suppose I should have started with that, Siobhan. Well I went to live with my granda, and as I said, I was delighted.

'I thought I'd have my own room instead of having to share with my three brothers. The first night my grandfather made me sleep in his bed. Horrible old smelly thing it was, with one of those mattresses filled up with feathers, they used to stick in my back. I can still smell that bed to this day.

'Anyway I woke up in the middle of the night and got a terrible fright. My granda had a hold of my willie and he was rubbing it and doing things with it. I didn't know what was happening to me.'

Ant paused, stroked his beard, his eyes became moist and little by little, overflowed in rivulets down his face.

'There was no one I could tell. I kept asking him to stop touching me like that. He wouldn't let me sleep in another room. The night was a nightmare, I used to spend all day dreading it. I got into the habit of sleeping on the floor next to the bed as soon as he went to sleep. Then I'd get up early and go and milk the cows.

'I tried everything to get him to stop but he'd call me a trouble-maker and told me that's why me ma got rid of me and he had to teach me a lesson.

'He made me do terrible things to him and to this day there are certain things I can't bear to smell because they bring back the memories.

'Like the smell of baked beans and I'd never be able to sleep if there was a pillow or anything with feathers in it. Everything down to the last cushion in our house has to be made with pure cotton.

'Then one day two men came to the farm to talk to my granda, they wore long black clothes and they were very nice. Granda called me into the kitchen and told me these men were Christian Brothers. They told me I could come and live with them and they'd give me schooling and I'd have a great time playing football and there were loads of lads the same age as myself.

'They showed us a big book with photographs in it. One I remember was of a big dining hall with the tables full of lovely food. Another was of a lovely bedroom which they said would be mine and just for me. And then there was a big football pitch and lovely gardens with flowers, apple and cherry trees.

'It was like a dream, it looked like it was heaven to me. I couldn't believe they wanted me to go with them and give me all those lovely things.

'My granda said it would be a great thing for one of his daughter's children to have an education and make something of himself. So my stuff was put in an old carrier bag and off I went with them. When I got to the Christian Brother's in Stillorgan, it didn't take me long to find out the truth.

'There was no table with all the food and fruit that was in the photographs. Oh they had it right enough, but we didn't.

'There was no bedroom, I slept in a room underground in the cellar, which was always cold and most of the time I worked on the farm and got very little schooling. Even if I was in the class I was too frightened to learn anything, I couldn't concentrate I was always expecting a thump.

'The Brother used to walk up and down the class and then he'd give you a box for nothing. One day the young lad who sat in front of me was boxed to the ground and kicked in the head. There was blood everywhere and a couple of his teeth were stuck to my shoe. I tell you I nearly died and I can still see that fellah lying on the floor unconscious. I don't know what happened to him, I never saw him again.

'The shaggers,' Bins said.

'They probably killed him and buried him, or burnt him in the boiler. Shaggin animals they were,' added Bins.

'Ah well it went on and on, it never stopped. The McGowan fellah was there, he was a fully trained Christian Brother by then. Like you Gerard, I've had a thing about red hair all my life because of him. I'd like to have scalped him!'

'Anyway one day, I was, maybe I was fourteen or so, I don't remember as I never had a birthday in there.

'Anyway I was way down in the orchard picking apples, there was a little shed down there, where we used to store them. Well yer man came up to me and caught me eating an apple. He dragged me into the shed and well, well'

Ant started to cry.

Siobhan stood up from her chair, and gave Ant a few tissues and a glass of water.

'Take your time Ant. If you want to stop then please stop.'

Ant finished his water and Cracker poured him another glass.

'Yer ok. Ant, yer among friends,' he said.

'Thank God,' Siobhan thought. A breakthrough with Cracker. There he was a few minutes ago ready to beat the living daylights out of poor Ant, now he's playing daddy to him.

The other men sat in silence. Gerard took a deep breath and ran his hands over his head, forgetting his comb-over, which now resembled the crest of a Cockatoo. Tom put his Arsenal scarf across his lap and stroked it. Bins looks behind him four or five times. Allan looked ahead, calmly keeping his eyes fixed on a light switch.

'Thanks Siobhan, everyone, I'm ok now. Sorry about that. Strange how we have all been able to let go of our sorrow in this room tonight, isn't it?'

They all agreed with him.

'Now where was I? Oh I know, the apple shed. He told me to get my trousers off, and I said I wouldn't. He had the leather hanging off his belt and I thought he was going to start on me with that thing and I was terrified. I kept saying, "I'm sorry Brother, 'I'm sorry Brother" and I didn't even know what I'd done. I thought if I said it enough times he'd leave me alone. I went down on my knees and begged him not to hit me.

'Then he took his penis out and told me to suck on it. I didn't understand and he told me to open my mouth and that's what I had to do.

'When he finished with me, he told me if I told anyone I'd go straight to hell because he's doing Gods work and nothing was a sin. But if I told anyone it would be a mortal sin and I'd go straight to hell.'

The room went silent.

'The next two years were torture for me, he'd beat me with the leather for nothing, and he raped me whenever he felt like it. I got to the stage I couldn't even talk anymore. I was too frightened to open my mouth.'

'We were allowed to write home once a month, but the letters had to be left open so they could read them before they were posted. 'I used to write that everything was wonderful, mind you I never got a letter back from my mammy and she never once visited me. Anyway it got so bad that one Saturday I was in confession with a priest called Father Brennan, now he was a nice old boy. Every time I went he used to give me penance of three Hail Mary's, I don't think he knew any more than that.

'He was that old he'd forgotten about the Stations of the Cross. I don't know what happened to me but I broke down roaring and crying and told him all that was happening to me. He didn't say much and gave me the three Hail Mary's as usual.

'I woke up in the middle of the night with a big hairy hand over my mouth. I was scared witless and for a minute I thought I was dreaming. Then I got such a box on the head I saw stars, I'm telling you, even though it was pitch black, I saw stars.

'I was dragged out of the bed and out into the fields and down to the farm.

'When I started to come round a bit I recognised the smell and then saw the red hair on his hands. It was McGowan and another Brother Walsh.

'Well they dragged me into the hay-shed and beat the living daylights out of me. They broke my wrist and to this day I have to look at that crooked hand and remember how it happened.

'Though my breathing and self-hypnosis has helped a lot with that. They were shouting and screaming at me. What a lying fucker I was, and how God would punish me for going into holy confession and telling a load of dirty lies to Father Brennan. Then when I was half senseless they dragged me into the chapel. One of the old Brother's had died that day and he was in the coffin in front of the altar with the lid off.

'They threw me in the coffin on top of him and put the lid on. They told me that if I made as much as a peep, they let me be buried alive with him.

'I don't know how long I was in there, I think I fainted. Anyway they came back and dragged me out, took me to the bathroom stripped me naked and made me stand under the freezing shower. Then they put my clothes back on me and reminded me if I said a word to anyone I'd be in the next coffin on my own.

'They took me to the old brother who ran the sick bay and told him they'd found me wandering around the back field and I must have been sleep-walking.

'They never even sent me to the hospital to sort my wrist out. The old Brother just put it between two planks and bound it up and put it in a sling.

Then one day I was outside McGowan's office I could hear him talking to someone and he was saying "the best thing to do with that fecker is to ship him off to Bindoon, get rid of him!" I knew they were talking about me and I had heard terrible story's about Bindoon.

Gerard interjected. 'I met a man at one of the compo meetings, he'd been sent there when he was ten. Shocking stories he was telling me unfeckin believable. It was in the Western Australia wasn't it?'

The men were sitting in shock and revulsion. Dezzie cried openly. Tom covered his head with his hands. Bins knocked the rings of each hand into the palm of the other. Cracker cracked the bones in his knuckles.

'When I heard that, I decided I had to escape from there. I knew it wouldn't be long until I became a professed Brother. Then they could send me anywhere. I took it into my head to run away.

'I slipped out in the middle of the night and ran to Stillorgan. I thumbed a lift. Imagine me standing on the side of the road at two in the morning, dressed in my cassock thumbing a lift? Anyway a lorry pulled up and I told him I had to get to Carlow my mammy was dying! He was a nice chap and drove me all the way to Carlow town, and I walked from there the couple of miles to my mammy's house!

'When I knocked on the door, she nearly died with the fright, she didn't even want me to come in. Between the jigs and the reels, she told me I was a disgrace and a shame to the family. She told me to get myself outta there and back to the Brothers; she said she didn't want any of the neighbours to see me because she told them all, I was getting an education and going to become a Christian Brother. She told me, I could sleep in the chair in the kitchen, but to get outta the house before she got up in the morning.

'I didn't tell her all that happened to me in that place, because she'd have given me a belt and called me a liar.

'Early the next morning I took an old suit belonging to my father. I even took his shoes, which were two sizes too big for me. I stole twenty pounds out of the tea-box my mother kept the rent money in, and I left.

I got a lift to Dun Laoghaire and jumped on the boat to Holyhead.

'To this day, I remember looking at Ireland going further and further away from me, feeling the cold, wind on my face and the freedom in my heart.

'Little did I know my heart and body were free but my mind would always be back with the Christian Brothers and that red head devil McGowan.

'It was years later when I was talking to one of my uncles, a brother of my mother; that I found out my granda had done the same to all his children, even to my mother. I could never forgive her, for sending me to that bastard, just a little boy I was. She must have known what he would do to me.

'She's dead now. God knows what secrets and lies she took to the grave with her. But I got the last laugh,' he smiled and stroked his beard.

'One night I went to the graveyard and pissed on her grave, after that I don't think even a dandelion 'ud grow on it.

'Good on ya Ant,' said Bins. 'If it was me, I'd have shat all over it.'

'I did all sorts of odd jobs when I arrived in England and then I applied to train as a nurse. I met Sheila, the love of my life. I told her bits of my story but I only told her about the beatings. I didn't have the courage to talk about the sexual abuse. I felt so much shame, as if it was all my fault; that I had asked for it in some way.

'Now with Siobhan's help I lost that shame, I see that devil as the paedophile he was and probably still is. Those fellah's never change, even if you cut their dick off, they'll use something else. It's more about power and control than sex.

'Now I work in an old people's home and I love it. My problem is I get very attached to them. You see most of them are inches away from dying. I protect them because you can get some weird people working in those places, and believe me they are as vulnerable as we were all those years ago. I always try to make sure they keep their dignity to the end, because I know what it's like to lose your own dignity.

'At the end of the day, the only two things that matter in this life is your integrity and your dignity.'

Ant sat quietly and stroked his beard. The room was quiet, everyone reflected and processing their own thoughts.

'Ant,' said Tom. 'Why dd... did ya... think th... that we'd nn... not want you to stay in the Group?

'Well I was part of them. I was a Christian Brother nearly!'

'Well I feckin tell youze.' Gerard shouted, 'if the rest of the lads in that feckin place were treated like you Ant; no wonder they came out as feckin crazy bastards and done the feckin same to us!

'The strange thing is lads,' said Cracker, speaking in a more mannered tone, 'woz it we all had that fuckin mad, red haired bastard play such a big fuckin role in our lives. How the fuck could something like that happen?'

'Sure we know now from the newspapers, don't we, that they moved the crazy shaggers around all over the place. Instead of kickin the shaggers out ta hell, they just moved them on to another institution to murder another one of us. Sure who shaggin cared? None of us had anyone who cared enough about us, or had the sense to find out wha was goin on!

'Did ya ever meet the likes of a doctor's son in one of them places? Sher of course ya shaggin didn't. If yer were in shaggin Letterfrack, yer mammy didn't even have the fare to get down there to have a look at yer.'

Gerard now joined in. 'Sure it wasn't just that. Even if ya had a feckin mammy and daddy, didn't they tink yer were in a lovely boarding schoel like the fecking Clongoes? They didn't know yer were in a feckin concentration camp.

'Look at the Artane boys band, shure weren't they famous all over the feckin world. Playing and marching at football matches and tings, in their fine uniforms. I was great at the piana, could play anything by me ear like. I asked them if I could join the band and they told me ta feck outta the place .Imagine saying something like that to a feckin sensitive lad like meself?'

Gerard stood up, making believe he had a piano strapped to his belly and started marching around the room pretending to play and sing the national anthem. The men fell about laughing. As usual Gerard had broken the tension, by simply being Gerard.

After calming down Ant started to talk once more.

'It was all about collusion, everyone knew. Sure some of you were taken to the Sunshine home in Balbriggan for a few days holiday. The whole of the town must have seen you on the strand. Don't tell me they didn't notice you were stick-thin and undernourished. Don't tell me they didn't see the bruises on you.

'What about the inspectors that used to come in every now and then. Don't tell me they didn't notice anything wrong. Sure anyone would have to be deaf and blind not to see the state of you or hear the stories.

'Nobody dared challenge the church, and the government was run by the bastard bishops. Who cared about a few young lads like you? The trouble was there wasn't just a few, there were thousands in the end. Look how dysfunctional we all were, when we came first to see Siobhan. What about all the rest of the poor buggers who didn't get any help? What about the children we have, how can they be normal when we were, and still are a mess? It was just one big, filthy conspiracy. Nothing more than trading children for money. For God's sake, ask yourself, who ran the farms and the workshops? The kids did.

'Now there's a big uproar, advertisements and people standing on corners with collecting boxes for the starving children in India and Third World countries. What about us? Didn't they starve you? Did they ever give you a toy or something to play with ? For God's sake weren't you just saying, the only time you got an egg was at Easter and the feckers had millions of feckin chickens!'

Ant was angry when he spoke about institutional abuse. He was exhausted from recounting his own story. He knew they were all empathic to each other, but the story was words, black and white. No one could grasp the use of each of their senses; the smells, the discomfort, the crying and screaming around them day and night. The freezing cold of the turf bogs in the winter, and most of all the constant fear and sense of high-alert; always waiting, waiting, waiting for next beating!'

Siobhan fingered her diamond pendant, as if she was unaware of what she was doing. After listening to Ant's account of his life and how he managed to turn it around, they were all exhausted.

'I think it might be an idea gentlemen to take a few minutes relaxation. You have listened to your own, and others, reflections of the maltreatment each of you experienced, you must be quite exhausted.

'I'm aware that many of you might have some memories coming into your minds that have been forgotten or hidden in your subconscious for some time. Would you like to take a few minutes break now, just to sooth, calm your minds and feelings?'

The men all agreed and settled their body's comfortably. Bins lay on the floor, propped himself on one elbow, looked around, then looked at Siobhan and relaxed.

Dezzie tried to shift himself into the foetal position but couldn't quite make it and settled for lying back in his chair. Gerard sat back, stretched out his long frame and started exhaling loudly, within seconds he was on his imaginary beach.

Only Allan was oblivious, to the calm which settled in the room. His mind was a mixture of all these men had been through, he wondered had his situation been different, would any of them had to have suffered those experiences. Would his story do them more harm? Would his secret expose them to more pain and anguish?

They listened to Siobhan sooth away their distress and sorrow. She took them into another place; a safe place, where they felt whatever they wanted to feel.

'Three, two, one. Take your time open your eyes when you're ready.' she said.

The men slowly opened their eyes.

'I a… always feel great a… after I do them re relaxation things,' Tom said.

Siobhan asked him if he felt like telling his story?

'Mm… might as well s… so,' he replied.

'There were four of us, three lads and one sister. I ww… was one of a twin, I'd identically we were. I tell yy… you when I looked at P… Paddy it was like looking in a m… mi… mirror and he felt the same.

'We used to h… have the same dreams and som… sometimes we didn't even need to s… speak because we'd knew what we were goin… to say b… before we even said it. We were six and the eldest Brother Ryan was nine.

'Af… after me little sister was born, me mm… mammy went a bit strange in the head and she was sent away to a hos… hosp… hospital, we never saw her again. The parish p… priest said me daddy cc… couldn't manage us all and t… told him we had to be sent away. Years later me d… daddy told me it bb… broke his heart, and he was never the same aa… again. Well I suppose yy… you wouldn't be would ya? He turned ta the drink and died from his liver giving up when he was sixty.

'Well me twin and meself ww… were sent to the Sisters of Charity in Drogheda and we didn't know until years eleven later that Ryan was sent to L… Letterfrack.

'Jayzus them sisters were d… devils. There was one called Sister Ignatious and she take the sk…sk… skin off your backside with a r… ruler or whatever else she could get hold of. 'She'd pull the h… hair off you and lift you up by th… the locks.

'I don't remember m… much about it, Siobhan says I… I've blocked it ow… ow… out and it doesn't matter; there's n… no need to even try to r… retriever those memories.

'One day the nuns told u… us we were too old to be w… with them anymore, we were me m… men now and had to go to a men's place.

'A big black c… ca… car took us a long w… way to a big building and dropped us off at the gates. The driver said "this is Artane" and made us walk up to the f… front door on our own and tell them who we were.

'It was terrible, pp… poor Paddy was crying and this big f… fellah in a black frock gave him a belt around the head and told him to be quiet.

'We were taken into the big of off… office. The main man told us where we were, th… that we'd be there fer… the rest of our l… li… lives, and if we didn't behave ourselves we get this thing wrapped around us. He h… han… handed me the leather and made me hit Paddy on the hand with it, then he mm… made Paddy do the same to me. We were r… roaring and crying and holding on to each other. Then this other big fellah in the black frock thing, came in and dragged us outta there. Then we were taken to the man for the new clothes, he did the same to the two of us, li… like you said Cracker, put his hand up our trouser leg and felt our w… willies. Then we were t… taken to a big room with about a hundred beds in it, and they gave Paddy a bed n… near the door and put me way down the other end. We were mi… miles away from each other. I'm imagine the two of us being separated like that?

'Sher,' Bins said, looking behind him.

'That's was what they did. Didn't I tell you? They divided and gave ya… conckers or whatever it was.'

'Divide and Conquer. Bins,' said Ant.

'Yeah that's what I'm after sayin! 'Bins retorted.

Tom continued. 'I suppose that was when m… me nightmares started.!'

'I'd I'd wake up screaming and hollerin in the m… middle of the ni… ni… night, the sweat pouring outta me and I'd wet the bed. Paddy u'd run up to me, hold me and try to calm me down. Then the b… big man, the Brother who sl… slept in the cubicler thing next to the dormitory, u'd come chasin in and b… be… beat the shite outta the two u'v us. He'd kick Paddy all the way back to his own b… bed. Look at me sheet, drag it off the bed and the then he'd.'

Tom became emotional, his voice broke. 'He'd wrap the pissy sheet arouwened me head and make me stand the rest of the night in the corner of the rooem.'

'The the n… next day, I'd be waiting all day fer me name to be called out to go to the off… of… office. Sometimes me name w… wo… wouldn't be called out 'till five o'clock. Me nerves were sh… shot ta pieces so they were.

When I'd go inta the office, ye yer man u'd call me n… n… names and say names about me mother I'd not understand; then he'd make me take me trousers down, he'd tell me to touch me to toes and he'd beat the shite outta me with the leather.

'The more I screamed, the mo… … more he did it. Then I… ler… lern… learned not to scream. I just used to put me mind somewhere else! I couldn't tell ya how many hun… hundreds of times that happened ta me because I was always p… pis pissing in the bed.'

'Fuckin bastard cowards so they were,' Cracker said.

'Th… they said I was n… no good in schooel!

Sh… shurre I w… w… was that te… terrified of that room, I couldn't even t… tink, let alone l learn anyting. They s sent me to the leather shop to m… me… mend shoes and m… m… make the leathers. I was no go good at that either because I was so small I had to stand o… on a box to reach the ta… table and I was always fallin off the bl… bloody thing.

Then they sent me to watch the turkeys. D… de… de youze remember the turkeys?'

The men nodded their heads or recognised in someway they did remember.

'Jayzus they were that b… b… big. Years later when I to… took me kids to the zoo, I saw an Ostrich and I was telling the kids it was a te turkey!

'I was terrified of them t… turkeys. Sure I was even terrified of the ch… chickens, but the turkeys… Jayzus to th… this day I'd die if I had to eat one.

'All them Brothers used ta play a g… ga… game. It was called Tom and the turkey tit. They'd g… get together and tell me to get in w… with the turkeys and bring them a turkey's tit! Shure, I didn't know what a tit was let alone a turkey's tit.

'Well they'd throw me in th… the p… pen and the turkeys 'ud be chasing me and I'd be screaming and sh… shouting, "where's the tit, which one yez is the tit? Tit. Tit. Tell me which one of youze is the tit?"

'Every time I tried to jump out of the p… p… pen the Brother's u'd throw me back in! They'd keep me at it 'till I'd f… fa… fall in a heap and not be able to move a muscle. Then the turkeys 'ud be pecking me and shitting on me. Then the bb… bastards taught me how to twist the turkey's neck and c… cut its throat. Well that was the f… fin… finish of me, because I used to vomit and faint. They'd throw a b… bucket of cold water on me, and make me get up and do another t… tur… turkey. Another thing they used ta do ta us was get us in the sh… sh… shower room. Jayzus ta this day, I c… co… couldn't go near a shower!

'They'd turn the w… w… water up real hot and ma… make us get in. We'd be hoppin around and t… tr… trying to jump out, a… and they'd kick us back in again. Th… th… then they'd do the same but with the co… cold water, we'd all be s scr… screaming. "P… please Brother, ple… please broth… Brother, we'll b… be g… goo… good lads!" Shure they didn't care they used ta piss themselves laughing.

'Then one night after I w… w… wet me bed, the Brother dragged me in… in… into the shower and made me strip meself. H… he threw me in and turned the fr… freezing water on. He lifted up the front of his black frock and pul… pulled down the zip of his trousers and took out his thing. He said "suck that and I'll let you outta there."'

Tom went quite, choked up and red in the face with shame.

'I tried to do it, b… bu… but I kept gagging and vomiting. He upped ww… with his fist and gave me such a punch in me, mouth, me t… t… two front t… teeth fell out on the flooar! There was bl… blood everywhere. He just told me ta clean meself up and ge… get back ta the bed. If I told anyone he said he'd knock the re… res… rest of me teeth out.

'I tell ya, I had a g gap in me mouth 'till I met the wi… wife, she took me to the den… dentist to get false ones made.

'The food was sh… sh… shite. As we were sayin, the only boiled egg I ev… ever got all those years was at E… Easter. The stew was full of fat and the tata's were bl… black. There'd be a loaf of bread on a ta… table between ten of us. I nev… never gotta bit, whoever wa… was strongest got the biggest bit. Ma… many's the ti… time I a… ate from the pig bins I was th… that h… hung… hungry. The worst was the b… breakfast, I'll never forget the porridge. I u… use… used to give mine away. Then they caught me and g… ga… gave me a beating, kicked me all around the refectory room so they did. I still couldn't eat the p… porridge and one day two of the Brothers caught me giving it away again.

'They'd drag dragged me inta the k… kitchen and laid me back on the big table.

They took big h… han… handfuls of porridge from the pot and they shoved it in me mouth and forced it down m… me throat. I couldn't breath, I couldn't ev… even scream, I thought I was going ta die. The porridge was even comin outta me nose like snot. Then they got me off the table and gave me a pun… punch in the stomach and the porridge flew outta me all over the kitchen. They called me a doirty fe… fec… fecker and made me scrub out the kitchen. I was that frightened I wet and shite meself. I was so frightened I couldn't even cr… cry anymore.

'That's when I started ta stutter, up until then I never had a stut… stutter. Ah shure ya know yer yerselves lads, youze all went trew it. God knows wha we did ta deserve all dat, but there ya are, it happened and that's that.'

'What happened to Paddy Tom?' asked Gerard.

Tom looked a little vacant for a moment.

'Well that's where… the red haired d… devil came in Ger… Gerard, and the thoughts of what hap… hap… happened to Paddy never left me 'till I had me treatment with Siobhan.

'The memories would kinda come in fl… flash… flashes. Honest ta God, I'd be d… do doin… me work or whatever and then I'd g… get a terrible flash, like a picture comin in ta me head an… and it was always the same one of Paddy.

'One day, he was called inta that McGowan's office like, and I waited outside the door, I kept tying and untying me shoe lace, like, p… pretending that's why I was there.

'I heard Pad… Paddy screamin and cryin inside. Shure no one p… paid any attention to a kid screamin or cryin 'cause it was goin on all day and n night.

'And then Pad… Paddy was kicked out the dooer and he walked in front of me and he had blood all over the back of his tr... trou... trousers and coming down his little legs. I thought he'd been given the leather and I w... w... was tryin to comfort him as best I could, but it wasn't like ya could put yer ar... arm around him or anyting 'cause if they caught you doin anyting like that, they'd tell ya you was 'scampin' and give ya a beatin.

'Anyway tha happened a good few times to poor Paddy and the then one d... d... day he stopped speaking. Wou... wouldn't say another w... w... word.

'Imagine the two of us, id... iden... identicaly twins, me with a stut... stutter and Paddy... not a word outta him.

'It was years later, I ff... found out that Pad... Paddy had been interfered ww... with by that mad bas... bast... bastard. I swore to meself every day since then, if I ever met him, I'd cut off his shagging prick.

'Anyway we g... got thrown outta there when we were just over fourteen. We went back ta me daddy b... but he was different. L... like he wasn't our daddy any more. I worked on the buildings fer a while, th... then I went to England and worked the rest of m... me life down the sewer. I became a sewer monkey in London.

'Jayzus,' said Bins, 'I didn't know they had monkeys workin in sewers! What the fek is a sewer monkey?'

They all looked at each other, trying to a get a clue about monkey's who lived in the sewers.

'It's 'a flusher. A man who cleans the se... s... sewers,' said Tom.

'Oh shit!' said Cracker.

'That's all I di… did fer over fo… foro… over forty years. I couldn't't read or write, so I hid me self away. My nightmare w… was always that I didn't't protect Paddy. I couldn't't save him from that r…. ed haired d… devil.

'I never fer fr… forgave me self for that.'

Tom burst into tears, he spread his hands over his eyes and the tears leaked through his fingers, trickling onto his Arsenal scarf. Siobhan walked over to Tom and brushed his hand as she gave him tissues.

'Tom, would you like to take a break?' she asked.

'N… no I'll be alright i… in a second Siobhan S… so… sorry lads.'

Cracker walked over to Tom and gave him a pat on the shoulder.

'You take your time there, Tom,' he said.

'Better out than shaggin in, I say,' said Bins and looked behind him.

Dezzie started to sob.

'Oh God help you Tom.'

He was interrupted by Cracker.

'Will you shut the f.'

Siobhan looked at Cracker and showed him the palm of her hand. Instantly he stopped.

Tom wiped the tears from his Arsenal scarf with a folded handkerchief.

'Paddy threw him himself under a train on our tw… twenty third birthday. I never c… celebrated me birthday since that day; I've only felt like half a man ever s… since.'

He looked down and quietly repeated himself, 'n… never c… celebrated a b… birthd since then.'

He looked around at everyone and smiled, the sadness disappearing from his face like a cloud passing over the sun.

'I met me wife, C… Cr… Chrissie at a St Patrick's D… Day dance in L… L… London.

'Her family are from Waterford. The best thing that ever happened tt… to me she was.

'We have three kids, grand kids, so they are. Never gave us a m… moments, worry. They all h… have th… their own families now.

'I never let them be bap… baptized. I never let them go into a ch… chur… church. I… in fact I taught them how to walk on the others s… side of the road when we saw a ch… ch… church. Ch… Chrissie didn't agree with this but she had to lump it. Th… there w was no way I'd let anyone who wore a c… cross, or a c… collar go near my k… ki… kids. When they were small and they'd ask me to help them with th… their homework, I used to pretend the teacher would be annoyed if she found out I did I it f for them.

'Chrissie would j… ju… jump-in then and tell them to come into th… the k kitchen and she'd help them. Shure I couldn't tell them about not being able to read or do sums. I even used to buy the pp… paper every day and pretend I was reading it.

'I told Ch… Chrissie about Artane. Mi mind you I didn't tell her e… everything.

'All those years I worked n… nights I was hiding. Hi… hi… hiding from meself, from me family and me nightmares.

'I worked in the sewers, it w… was probably the worst job in the world. It m… might have been shit to everyone else, but to me it was me bread and butter. I felt like a rat after P... Paddy died and I lived every night like was one.

'Then a c cu couple of years ago we won a b bit of money on the lottery.

'I didn't want to come back to Ireland but Chrissie's dr... dream was to l... live near her family. G... God knows she worked ha... hard enough for it, she always had a p... part time job working in Tesco. Never g... gave it up, even when the kids left school. So in the e... en... end we came back to I... Ireland and bought a little place in Waterford; not big mind, but enough room for all the kids to visit and the grand-kids.'

'Ah,' Bins said, 'sher wasn't that great. Sher you deserved a bit of luck so you did.'

'I... sup... suppose I couldn't settle. I couldn't sleep at night after all those years wer... working nights, and I'd only sleep for a couple of hours during the day. I had nothing to do. Chrissie got a part time job in the lo... lo... local Tesco's but I did nothing except think.

I still had the ni... ni... nightmares, only they were d... daymares. I got d... d... depressed and the doctor gave me tablets, but shure they made me worse. You see. All those y... years down the sewers, I had a place to h... hi... hide. Now, I had nowhere to hide, it meant I had to meet p... p... people and to talk to pe... pee... people, I was scared sh... sh... shitless.

'One night, I wa... was lying in bed and the fright took o... over me. I took all me d... depression tab... tablets and sat in a chair waiting to die. I remember saying in me head "I'm coming Paddy, I'm coming, it won't be long now."'

Cracker bowed his head and supported it with his hands, his elbows on his knees. The tears were running down Gerard's cheeks, his nose was running, but he didn't seem aware of it. Dezzie curled himself up in the chair and assumed the foetal position. Ant lowered his eyes and gently stroked his beard. Bins kept looking behind him.

'Jesus Christ, Tom, God love ye!' Cracker said.

'Well I got as si… si… sick as a dog. I was vom… vomit… vomiting so hard I was shitting me self at the same time. After that I felt wa… worse. I f… f… felt I was the biggest co… cow… coward and loser that was ever b… born. I went our out inta th… the garden and found a bi… bit of an ould r… rope in th… the shed. Then I w… went to the big ap… apple tree and threw it a few times over and around the b… big biggest branch.

'Then I went back to the k… kit… kitchen and got a chair, made a loop in the rope and put it around my n… neck.

'I remember looking up at the stars and f… fee… feeling a strange kind of peace. I must have kicked the ch… ch… chair away, and I didn't remember anything after that.'

Tom leaned forward, put his head in his hands and moved it from side to side.

'I woke up in Waterford Regional Hospital, in plaster from me knees to me neck. They told me I was unconscious for three days. Sher I d… don't remember a thing. Chrissie was standing over me and she called me all the names under the sun. I never knew, she even knew that kinda language.

'God love her,' said Gerard. 'God love her, she must have got a terrible fright!'

'I'll never fer... fer... forgive meself,' Tom replied, 'for p... put... putting her through that... She ca... came down to get a glass of water and saw the back door wi... wide open and me in a he... heap under the apple tree. The branch on the apple tree ha... had b... broken, and when I fell to the ground, I broke me ba... ba... back'

'God all mighty Tom,' said Dezzie.

'Well I was in the hospital for a good few weeks. I had to see a psychiatrist, but shurre I didn't tell him anything except that I was depressed. Then I was moo... moved to the National Rehabilitation Hosp... Hospital in Dun Laoghaire. I had to see a... another sys... psychiatrist there and she was l... lu... lovely. It was her that told me I had to get hel... help. That's when I started to see Siobhan.

'Sh... she... she got it all oooo... out of me, and it didn'y take her long either. Sh... shurre I w... was bring... bringing things u... up th... that were ev... even frightening th... the life outta me, me self. It wasn't easy an and I did a lo... lot of cryin and boxin me self with with me fists. Shurre you no n know yer... yerselves lads.

'Chrissie and I came here together at first, I w... was f... frightened to come on me own! Then we would come separately and wait fer each other.

'Ya see pp... poor Chrissie nearly had a nervous breakdown. One minute she was a... angr... angry and the next minute she was sad. She couldn't s... sleep because she was ter... terrified I'd get up in the night and do the same thing again.

'Well there's no chance of that now. I'm as happy as Larry and so is Chrissie. Me kids were very good, and now they un... un... understand that when they used ta ask me ta help them with their ho... home... homework why I'd tell them "Go and ask yer mammy." Sher, I couldn't read or write a word.

'We com... come here every week and make a day of it. We go to Bewleys in G... Grafton street for a big Irish breakfast and then a lovely walk on the G... Green. Sometimes we stay with Chrissie's sis... sister,' he said

Chapter 10

THE MEN sat quietly, each one of them lost in Tom's drama, and comparing it with their own experiences. There was no comparison. Each of them had experiences related to the others, but at the same time, incomparable with the effects they had all suffered.

Cracker asked Tom, 'what happened to yer other Brother? Ryan was it,' he said.

'Yes Ryan.'

'Well, he was in Letterfrack and somehow ended u... up in Daingean. I heard. I heard he was living in England down Camden way, but I was never able to find him.

'Den one day, Chrissie was readen the newspaper, sh... she always used to rea... read bits and pieces te me.

'All of a sudden she jumped up outta the chair and shouted "Jesus, Mary and Joseph!"

'Eejit, th... that I am. I th... thought we musta won the l lottery again, or sometink.

'Anyway she says to me, "Tom. I tink I found yer brudder!"'

'She showed me a pic picture in the paper, now he was a lo... lot older like, but I'm nearly sure it was him. It was the i... im... image of him.

'"Read it te me, read it te me," I asked her.'

'Well I tell ya, we both nearly fainted, we didn't know what to do, so we did nothing.

'If it was him. Then he was one of terrorists shot in the bomb attack in London. If it was him, he was a mem... member of the IRA.

'So I suppose w... wh... whatever happened to him in Letterfrack and Daingean, it sent him over th the edge. I don't know. Who knows, whatever it was.... he took it to the grave with him. G... God rest his s soul.'

'How could anyone come out of Daingean with his head straight. Those Oblates were the worst sadists ever. The way they leathered you caught the crack of yer arse, it would take two of them to beat you. One with his foot on your shoulders to make sure you couldn't move and the other laying into you 'till he nearly collapsed with the exhaustion.'

Bins looked behind and said: 'sher doncha know?'

'Sure look at the likes of Martin Cahill,' Ant said.

'Another product of the institutions. 'Whoever came out of those places and went to a university?' said Ant.

'The only fuckin university they went to was Mountjoy!' replied Cracker. He looked at Siobhan, as if she would verify his statement.

Bins looked behind him, then shouted.

'Sher doncha know?'

Siobhan looked at both Ant and Cracker.

'It wasn't so much that the Institutions were breeding grounds for criminals. You can see by your own lives that this was rare. Many of the children put into these places, were innocent of any criminal behavior. Okay some of them had been convicted of minor offences prior to being sent to them.

'When Edmund Rice had the idea to open a safe place, for children who were deprived. His perception was to take them off the streets, give them an education, feed and take care of them. The concept was good.

'Unfortunately the fanatics who ran and worked in these places destroyed Rice's ideal.

'Had they been doing the job they were paid to do, caring, educating and nurturing the children, it would have given them by example the skills they needed to create an alternative way of living.

'Had they encouraged the children to succeed, to understand the pleasure in success and achievement, Rice's conception would have been a huge success. They had the power to change the outcome of so many children's lives. Don't forget the Christian Brothers ran many schools and had an excellent reputation for their teaching skills.'

Gerard interrupted her.

'Only if your father was a doctor, or your mother ran a Post Office'

Dezzie interrupted Gerard.

'What happened to your baby sister Tom?'

'I never fou… found out. I as… asked me da a few times, but he wouldn't talk about it. God knows if she's a… alive or d… dead, or where she is. To tell y you the truth, and I'm ashamed to sit here and s… sa… say it.

'I didn't try to find h… her. I have so much sh… sha… shame attached to Paddy and me me… memories and what with th… the nightmares and everything. I don't think I could cope if I found out sh… she went through the same as us.

'I just don't want to h… hear it. I'm sc… scared of knowing and I'm s scared of no not knowing so I just try to b… blank it out.

'Siobhan says when I'm r… red… ready. I 'll be red… ready. Everything comes in its own time. I believe in that. She says I've been through enough and don't need to take anything else on b… board.

'I'm a different man n… now, I have a life. Be be… before all I had was a habit. Hiding and sc… scurrying around in a s… sew sewer like a rat. I feel I'm l lu… lucky; if it wasn't for an old apple tree, I wouldn't't be here to t tell the t… tale.'

'Ah sher don't you know?' said Bins, looking behind him.

The room went silent, each of them lost in their own thoughts. Suddenly and without any warning, Cracker stood up. He started walking around the space that was available to him. His hands clenched and unclenched into fists. He became more and more agitated.

Siobhan looked at him with concern. Knowing Cracker could not sit when he was agitated, she was more concerned with regard to the lack of space he had right now.

Dezzie shifted in his chair, his eyes fixed on Cracker's every movement, as if he is waiting for a tiger to spring on him.

Cracker groaned sounding like a wounded animal. All eyes followed him.

Siobhan stood up slowly and moved into Cracker's space, without touching him she looked him in the eyes and spoke to him.

'Are you alright Cracker?'

He made eye contact with her, but it was as if he didn't see her.

'Cracker, do your breathing.'

Siobhan started to inhale slowly and exhale through pursed lips, as if she is blowing through a straw. Cracker took a deep breath and did the same.

Dezzie, Tom and Ant looked nervously at him; their eyes fixed on hid every movement.

Gradually, his body relaxed. Cracker looked around him as if he had arrived at a destination he didn't recognize.

Siobhan swept the room with her eyes.

'I think gentlemen, this might be a good time to go out into the garden and do some deep breathing.'

All of them relaxed and make quickly for the door. Siobhan walked close beside Cracker, talking softly to him. He smiled at her and nodded his head.

Outside Ant lighted a cigarette and inhaled.

'Will you give me one them Ant?' asked Gerard. Ant handed one to him. Gerard's hands shook slightly. Ant lit the cigarette for him. Cracker looked at the two of them.

Gerard nearly jumped out of his skin as Cracker came up behind them.

'Them things, I'll kill yez!'

He smiled at the two of them. As he walked away, Gerard whispered to Ant.

'Feckin die from this, then have me head torn off by that mad fecker.'

Ant didn't reply.

It was cool outside, the fresh air smelt sweet; it regenerated them. None of them wanted to speak they just enjoyed the silence. Following Siobhan's lead they inhaled and exhaled gently.

Dezzie picked up a white rose which had fallen from a bush and handed it to Siobhan. She smiled at him. Siobhan returned inside and one by one they trailed behind her.

'Well I tell yez,' said Cracker.

Dezzie jumped at the sound of Cracker's voice, the others turned their heads and looked at him.

'I say, I tell yez. I didn't't want to fuckin come to this meeting. Siobhan will tell ye. But I tell yez lads, I'm proud to be one of yez. I thought I was the only man in the world them bastards ruined. After listening te yez and all yez have been through, well I just want te say.' He stopped right then. Tears appeared in his eyes.

'I'm proud to be one of yez, and we can all hold our fuckin heads up and be proud we survived it.'

'Here here,' said Gerard.

'Me too,' said Dezzie.

'Ah well,' said Bins. 'That's life I suppose.' Ant said

he was proud to have found such great new friends. The others nodded in agreement.

Siobhan looked at them.

'I would just like to say, as we seem to be starting a mutual admiration society here. That it has been an honor to work with all of you and I thank you all for giving me the opportunity.'

All except Allan looked slightly bashful, but proud.

'Now Bins, what about you? Would you like to share your story now?'

'I suppose I might as well.'

'I was one of seven we lived in the Liberties, shurr there were that many of us me mammy never even knew who the half of us woz. 'Shurr it was that bad, there were 4 or 5 to a bed. One night I remember one of us crying in the night and me mother came in ta see wha was goin on.

'"Which one of yez are makin all that racket for fecks sake?" she says. And a voice from the middle of the bed said: "It's me missus, I wanna go home te me mammy!"

'Jayzus, wasn't it the young fellah from down the road.'

The men started laughing, the atmosphere in the room lifted, they all seemed more relaxed.

'Me Da was a coal man, when he was sober, when he was drunk, he was a shaggin uldd fart. Me ma used to send us down to Flaherties on a Friday night ta rob his pay packet off him before he drank the lot. Then he'd get home and be cursing he was robbed, he'd say ter her, "give me piece a bread woman or I'll ate the child?" She'd tell him he could eat the shaggin lot of us; there wasn't as much as a pick on any of us.'

Dezzie started to giggle and Gerard nearly fell off the chair laughing. Bins was enjoying himself. It was a new experience for him to be able to make people laugh. Usually he terrified them, or made them shit their pants.

'I tell ya we'd get the odd clip or box, but shurr everyone did in those days. We were all great runners and shurr the mammy and daddy u'd never have been able to catch us once we were outta the door.

'But dere again, it was a hard life for them but shurr there was no malice in them. We were poor enough; we had one suit between us boys and an old hand-me-down of me granddaddies.

'So two of us'd go to de first mass on a Sunday, and then the next two u'd take the suits and go to the second Mass. One of us always stayed at home, me mammy would toss a coin u'd always have to stay at home.

'Ah she was a prowed woman, God rest her soul. She made frocks fer the girl's outta old tablecloths and matching bows for their hair. 'She even made school bags out of any ould bit of a sack. Ah shirr life was hard but wasn't it hard fer everyone?'

'Den one day I was about eight; I was walking trew de park and dere was an ould bit of a bike lying on the grass, not doin anything. Shurr it didn't't belong ta anyone an I picked it up and walked it hoam. Shurr I didna know how to shaggin ride it. I was a little sparrow of a lad, the ting looked like a big butcher's yoke wid a basket on de front.

'Anywayas I was near the Liberties and de next ting a big hand picked me up off me feet from the back of me collar. I nearly shite me self. Wasn't it the big hairy shaggin Garda, Sergeant Malone. Sher he was the feckin scourge of the Liberties that fellah.

'He asked me "Whose'is the bike?" And I told him "shurr it's my shaggin bike."

'He gave me a clip that knocked me head sideways. I tell ya me eyes nearly ended up at the back of me head instead of at the front.

'Ah shurr he draggded me hoam and me ma gave me a belt and then she gave the Garda a belt fer given me a belt. Then I tauld him "shurr I'd only borrad the bike fer the day."

'Anywayas I was dragged down to the Garda station, screaming and roarin crying, and me ma behind me screamin and roarin curses at yer man.

'Behind me ma, de brudders and sisters shouten curses at him too. Jaysus, it was like a shaggin circus, and yer man was tryin to walk the bike at the same time, then he fell over himself.

'That made him in worser humor so he picked me up and trew me in the basket, hopped on de shaggin bike and pedaled off with de whole family chasin after us,' said Bins, who once again, looked over his shoulder.

'Ah well, den I was in de Children's Court and all me family were dere, even me da, and he was sober fer once in his life. The judge sentenced me to

Marlborough House and then to Upton. Me ma was screamin and cryin and callin the judge an ould fart and who did he tink he was, the feckin hanging udge? Me da lost it and shouted out he wasn't the shaggin hangin Judge he thought he was shaggin Jaysus Christ. The brudders and sisters were all roarin and cryin and I shite meself.

'Well dat was dat. I was in that shaggin place Marlborough Howes for a couple of weeks beein touched up by every shagger, then I ran away. I ran home so I did!

'Shurr I wasn't't hoam for two minnits before de guards came knockin on the door for me.

Me ma shoved me under de bed and opened the door. Christ be ta God yer wud have thought I was the shaggin head of de IRA!

'Foive of de shaggers came in, they found me and dragged me out from under de bed and carried me kickin and screamin back to Marlborough House. Dey kept me one nigh dere and sent me off to Upton de next day.

'Well I tell ya, those Rosminian brudders u'd knock those shaggin Christian Brudders inta cocked hat any day. I got da leather de foirst day just as a warning what u'd happen to me if I as much as opened me shaggin gob. Well Oi tell yez I hated them shaggin bastads, and I wouldna keep me shaggin gob shuh.

'Two of the shaggers got holda me one night and had me hangin by me legs outta the top winda. Screamin at me, so they were to keep me gob shuh or dey'ed drop me. Well I kept me gob shuh 'till dey pulled me in. Denn I called dem shaggin bastards and dey beat me all over the place, they jumped on me shaggin leg and broke it.

'I tell ya, I was wheeled arowened de schooel for six months in a shaggin pram and when one of the wheels came off de pram they wheeled me abouh in a shaggin wheelbarra. 'Look at me leg, it's still shaggin crooked?' He pulled up his trousers and showed them his leg.

Cracker looked disgusted.

'I'd shoot every fuckin one of them, so I would.'

Bins winked at Cracker and then looked behind him.

'Shurr I already did one of dem Cracker; buh I keep it ta me self. Least said sooner mended ugh? Except fer the shaggin leg!

'Anyway dey got fed up wid me there and I was sent up to Artane. Shurr Artane was a palace in comparison wid dat hell hole Upton and dose Rosminian shaggers.

'Anywayas three toimes I ran away from Artane, ah shurr dey knew I had nowhere ta go, but me ma's and dey always got me back.

'Everytime dey got me back de stood me in de middle of the square and beat the shite outta me. Dey'd shave every bit u'v hair off me head in front of all the lads. Oh yes all de lads had to watch tha.

'Den de worse thing was, de big boy's u'd have a go at me and kick me all arouwened de field, because every time a lad ran away they'd cancel the film they had for that week.

'Da yer remember dere was a film every now and den? Well dey'd stop thah if someone ran away, just so as the big lads u'd beat the shite outta the runner," said Bins, again looking behind him.

'Ah shurr it was hell on shaggin earth in dere.

'The McGowan fellah got howeled off me and did the same ta me as he did to youze. Jayzus the smell of him. I yoused ta hied under the shaggin beds, buh that fella u'd find me and drag me owt. I got so as I didn't't shaggin care anymore. I put me mind somewhere else. Like I was on a horse, you know out in de wild west, chasing them Indian people.

'To dis day, I can't sleep in a shaggin bed, I don't feel safe. I can only sleep under de bed. 'My front teeth were knocked out as well,' he said to Tom.

'Most of de lads in dat place were walkin abouh wid no front teeth, an all of dem pretendin dey lost dem playin football. But I tell ya, if I ever see tha red-haired devil, I'll shaggin swing fer him. He took away me manhood so he did, and I tell ya someone has ta pay for tha.

'Den 'cause I was a runner dey put me on a train wid two of the biggest gorilla brudders dey had and carted me off to shaggin Salthill.

'Jayzus ya couldn't do a runner from Letterfrack sher it was like bein in the wilds of shaggin Africa. I spent the rest of me toime digging shaggin peat.

'Jayzus I hated that place. There was a shaggin nurse dere dat kept given me a bath and a brudder standin watching her and him playing wid himself while she was playin wid me. It had a terrible effect on me sex life I tell ya.

'I used ta hide from dem all and the best place was in de toilet. I'd leave the dooer open a crack and stand on de toilet .That way, dey couldn't see me legs if dey looked under the dooer, 'cause the dooer was a little bit open dey would tink no one was in dere.

'Mind yez, since den oive never been able to piss without standin on a chair If anyone of me family comes inta the bathroom when I'm in there they gets flattened. I tell yez, beein in dem places had a terrible cyclological effect on me head.'

He looked at Siobhan.

'Didn't it Siobhan, she she'll tell yez. It did, didn't it Siobhan?'

'Yes Bins, it did,' said Siobhan, encouraging to say more.

'Whah was it yer were telling me Siobhan about that trimatical distress thing?'

Siobhan had no wish for the group using this time for a session but felt it would be appropriate to explain a couple of facts to them. They had heard it before in their one-to-one sessions with her. However, hearing it within a group situation, might reinforce why the difficulties they had were as persistent and unremitting as they were.

All eyes now turned on Siobhan. Gerard and Bins especially, loved it when she explained facts to them. When she could answer the why, it made their fears less.

Cracker didn't give a shit as to the why's and wherefores. As far as he was concerned, he was a bastard because unnatural things happened to him as a child. Whoever did those things to him would pay sooner or later. He would make sure of that. For Cracker, revenge, was the best medicine.

'Living twenty four hours a day,' Siobhan explained, 'with the extreme fear, and constantly thinking you were going to die, is the main factor for Post Traumatic Stress Disorder. Day after day you were exposed to violence. If it wasn't happening to you, you were watching it happen to someone else. 'Your mind and body were on constant high alert, waiting, waiting, and waiting. You heard Tom say, how he had to wait all day for his name to be called; he knew he would have to endure another beating for wetting his bed.

'When you are in a state of extreme fear, when you think you are going to die, or someone else is going to die, the body goes into what we call, "fight or flight."

'You were little children, you couldn't fight and you couldn't run away. Bins, for instance was constantly looking for a place to hide. He discovered the toilet was his safe haven. Bins still consciously believes the toilet is his safe place. Dezzie believes his safe place is in the cupboard. Gerard found his was in a bottle of Jamesons. You all found a haven.

'Then of course there was the deprivation. You were all deprived of toys, education, love, nurturing and, any kind of positive affirmation as well as nutrition, hygiene and normal medical facilities.'

They looked at each other. Bins gave Tom a gentle dig in the arm. Tom acknowledged it. 'She's right, th…. that's how it was,' he said to Bins, who now looked about.

'Ya see lads, no wonder I grew up into a shaggin nut-case of a man. An I tell ya,... and I'm ashamed ta say it, I did de same ta me owen kids. I beat the shaggin shite outta dem!'

'Tell me Bins,' said Cracker. 'Why de ye wear them fuckin rings, shurr they're bigger than your fuckin fingers?'

'Well I tell ya Cracker,' Bins replied, as he fingered his rings.

'Ever since I came outta dem places I have to have things in me hand. I used to carry a bunch of pennies, then a bag of nails. Then one day I saw a gangster filim and yer man had them knuckle-duster things on. Bejayzus, I thought they were great things. But don't ye know it's against the law to wear them. It isn't against the law to wear these.'

Holding his hands in the air, he spread his fingers displaying the enormous, chunks of paraphernalia. Allan viewed them with distaste.

Tom said: 'I'd be w... worried now about th... them Bins. If you turned over in bed you might cut yer nose o... off. Sher I wouldn't mind cutting me shaggin nose off Tom, me sinus's are at me so much.'

'Everyone of dem was made special fer me. Shurr da ya not see me looking behind me self all the time, that's called a tik so it is. Dat's because the shagger's were always grabbin me from behind. Now I always have ta sit facing a door and keep looking behind me. This is the way I pretext me self.'

Bins stood up and walked about the room, whistling as if he hadn't a care in the world. All of a sudden one hand shot up in the air. Like lightening, he twisted his body and smashed his fists into the imaginary face and body of someone behind him. Calmly, as if nothing had happened, he put his fingers up to his face, as if they were a smoking gun he blew on them.

Dezzie was shocked at the speed of the imaginary violence which had just taken place. Ant abhorred violence, either physical or verbal. He turned his face away and looked out of the window.

Gerard remarked that he'd never seen the likes of it.

'Bins you should be in one of those Chinese films. What are called? King Phew!'

'Ah sher Gerard,' Bins replied, 'I never use dem much dese days, I just feel safer with dem on. Now when I was younger, it was a different story. I had to use a toothbrush every week to get rid of the skin and blood stuck in them. I never take them off, day and night, dey are on me fingers. De the only time dey come off is when I clean dem. I was in the hospital one time to have an operation on me ear, and the nurse told me to take dem off.

'"I will in me arse," I told her. These shaggin things will never come off. Yer operating on me shaggin ear not on me fingers ye ould bitch.

'When I woke up, I was wearing the biggest pair of bright yella Marigold gloves ye've ever seen. Sher the surgeon was frightened I'd give him a clatter while I was under the ana… anna… sthetic stuff.' He looked behind him, once more.

'Bins' said Gerard, 'you went through a lot fer a little fellah. I don't know how ya survived it! shurr what happened to me was nothing by comparison!'

Dezzie agreed with Gerard and with the exception of Allan, the rest of the men murmured similar, sympathetic remarks. Bins had finished his disclosure. Siobhan turned to Allan. His was the last disclosure in the group. The room was quiet, the atmosphere heavy. The group were dazed, saturated with each other's pain. The realization had dawned, that each one of them was not the only victim and not the only survivor.

Siobhan accepted she had taken a risk bringing them together. So far the positive outcome was worth that risk.

Allan would be the decisive factor. It was now too late to turn back. Physically and emotionally she was starting to feel exhausted. Ethically, she was aware; she should have brought at least one psychologist to the meeting to assist her.

A recovered memory from one of her clients would blow the room apart. The ferocity and continuous descriptions of childhood abuse would be too traumatic for anyone to accept.

For her gentlemen, as she liked to call them, her theory was that self-isolation had imprisoned them in the past. Opening the door of the cage would enable them to fly.

Siobhan looked at Allan.

'Allan, would you like to share your experience with the group?' she asked.

Allan presented a calm exterior. He had been deeply moved by every account he had heard so far, but he was worried.

'Siobhan. When you asked me to come along to this group, I didn't understand why it was so important to you, and why you thought it would be important for me. Now I do, and thank you for giving me the opportunity to attend,' he said.

Bins shifted in his seat and looked behind him. Seeing the other men looking at Allan, he imitated them. He hadn't been concentrating. Tomorrow, he would visit his son in the Joy. He hated the thought of it. The doors clanging behind him, the smell, and the noise, it reminded him too much of Letterfrack.

Suddenly he had a flashback, a black and white picture of a forced sexual initiation by three inmates.

'Bastards, shaggin bastards,' he blurted.

His conversation with himself took the role of two people, Bins and Bins.

'Shure you don't have to go if it makes you feel that bad.'

'Yes you do, you put Martin in there!'

'Well you did it, for his own good.'

'No you didn't, you just wanted the shagger out of the house.'

He felt the sweat starting to ooze out of every pore, the slow trickle of his own fluid down the back of his neck.

'Oh Jayzus, not now, not now,' he thought.

His tongue was dry, his throat felt as if it was closing and his heart hammered so hard in his chest, the sound nearly burst his ear drums. He felt the icy chill creeping up his arms and his legs began to tremble.

'I'm going to die, I'm going to shaggin die,' he thought.

Siobhan glanced at him and automatically registered his silent, internal screams.

'I'm sorry Allan,' she interrupted.

'I should have done this before you started. There's too much tension in the room it's suffocating us. Gerard can you open all the windows and doors please?'

'Sher of course I can Siobhan.' He jumped up, delighted to be asked.

'Everyone take a deep breath, through your nose to the count of seven and exhale out, that's it, you know how to do it, as if you are blowing through a straw. Bins you get on the floor and do it. Cracker you stand just outside in the fresh air. Tom sit up straight, you can't do it bent over like that. Dezzie get out of the fetal position and stand up please. Move around if you want to.'

The pallor began to lift from Bins face as he inhaled and exhaled. He looked at Siobhan and nodded a silent thank you to her. After a few minutes they all looked more alert and refreshed.

Siobhan focused on Bins. She looked at him; he was sitting on the floor, his elbow supported on a chair, his head lying over one arm. He looked calmer now, he had stopped panting, his breath slowly evening out and coming in natural waves. The tension had come out of his body and his limbs were relaxed. Not wanting to place any unwanted attention on Bins, she turned to Tom.

'Are you okay Tom?'

'G…great thanks Siob…Siobhan,' he replied.

'How about you Bins?' she said.

'Great Siobhan thanks,' he grinned at her.

'Okay. Ant can you get some more cold water out of the fridge please, and everyone drink a glass.'

Ant did as he was asked.

'My God,' he thought. 'She has eyes in the back and sides of her head; I thought Bins was going to pass out on us.'

Cracker, still standing between the door and the outside patio, looked puzzled. He slowly sipped his water, looking under his eyelids at both Siobhan and Allan.

'Who the hell is this guy? There's no way he went through the same system as the rest of us. What the hell has he got to offer?

Maybe,' he thought, 'he's another psychologist and is going to give us a load of bull-shite psychobabble.'

'Okay gentlemen; take your seats again please,' Siobhan said, 'I'm so sorry to interrupt you Allan.'

'No problem Siobhan, we all needed that break,' he said.

She smiled encouragingly at him. 'When you're ready.'

The men settled down and looked expectantly at Allan.

Allan sat back comfortably in his chair, crossed his legs and folded one manicured hand gently on top of the other. He assumed a stance which left the others in no doubt, that this was a serious man; well versed in the art of conversation and getting his point across briefly and succinctly.

'My parents were separated when I was two and I lived with my mother. I saw my father occasionally, he was a High Court judge and attaining that position left him very little time for anything else.'

'Jayzus,' said Bins, looking behind him, 'I hope I haven't been up before him.'

'Nor me,' said Cracker, looking at Siobhan accusingly.

Allan smiled at Cracker's and Bins remarks and continued.

Siobhan knew what Cracker was thinking but was glad he was showing some restraint.

She was worried about Dezzie. He was the one out of all of them, who might abreact with the disclosures Allan was about to make.

'I don't remember much about the first few years of my life,' said Allan. His accent was in stark contrast to the others, English with just a slight trace of Irish.

'Like yourselves my mind has a safety catch. Thank God it can close down to the unbearable, however my body still remembers. Like you Dezzie, sometimes I get strange feelings, sometimes I go into myself, it's as if I am in a tunnel, not quite sure where the exit is and I don't know if I should go forwards or backwards.'

Dezzie, unused to being referred to sat up and shook his head.

'Thank God someone else understands that feeling,' he thought.

Allan continued. 'My mother had a brother who would stay with us from time to time. I remember I used to hate it when he arrived. I would try to hide but

I could never find a place they wouldn't find me. I was terrified when they got together. I didn't understand for a long time why I had those feelings.' Allan shifted slightly in his chair and looked at Siobhan.

'Are you quite sure about confidentiality Siobhan?'

Siobhan looked around at the men one by one.

'Do I need to remind you all about confidentially?' She paused.

'Nothing you have heard tonight, goes outside this room, it's not even up for discussion between each other.'

'Well I…I'll go to my grave with what I've heard here tonight,' Tom stuttered, as he looked at Ant, Gerard, almost as if he was speaking for both of them.

'Sher we're not thick fer Gods sake!'

Ant looked at Gerard and then over at Siobhan.

'Not one of us is going to breathe a word of what has been said in this room Siobhan.' Ant stared explicitly at Allan, 'put your mind at rest Allan, it isn't going to happen.'

Dezzie shook his head vigorously. Bins looked behind him. 'No shaggin way,' he added.

Cracker flexed the bones in his hands; the noise startled Tom who was sitting beside him.

'Jayzus if I hear anything repeated I'll fuckin tear the f.'

'Ah here we go with the cowboy threats,' remarked Gerard, never one to miss an opportunity.

'Shurrup you, ye tap-dancing eejit.'

'That's enough,' Siobhan said looking at them both sternly.

'Do you want to continue Allan?' Allan nodded his head.

'I was five when I went to live with my father, I never saw my mother or uncle again, and I don't ever remember asking about them.

My father sent me to Willow Park, and then onto his old school Clongowes, I was a weekly boarder and spent every weekend with my father.

'It was a very Catholic environment but the Jesuits were fair and brilliant teachers, I enjoyed it there. I loved the smell of the old castle and the tales of the ghosts that haunted the place.'

'Ghosts?' interrupted Gerard. 'What. Real Ghosts?'

'Yes,' Allan replied, 'if ghosts are real, there were a few of them Gerard.

'There were a lot of accidents outside the main gates. People often said, they swerved to avoid a young boy crossing the road, but there was never a sign of the child. Also many people said they had seen a coach and horses driving past the gates late at night.'

'Ah Jayzus now, I think I'd rather have a slap or a box than experience that,' said Gerard.

Allan smiled.

'The only problem I had at school was….I didn't like sports. Everyone else was rugby and cricket crazy but I just never saw the point in running myself ragged after a ball. My great love was maths.'

Gerard interrupted again.

'Sher the only thing I know about arithmetic is my once times table, one times one is one, one times two is two….'

Siobhan frowned, 'Gerard please stop interrupting Allan.'

'Ah Jayzus me and me big mouth again go on Allan.'

'Well to cut a long story short, I got all A's in my leaving Cert and went onto to Trinity where I did my BSc and MSc in Mathematics. My father then suggested I go to Harvard Business School in the States to do my PHD.'

Gerard put up his hand. Allan looked at him calmly and said, 'Yes Gerard, what is it?'

'I don't understand what all those alphabet things are yer talking about Allan, and I bet the other lads don't either but they are too afraid to put up their hands.'

Ant shifted forward in his chair.

'We are not all thick Ger, all those alphabet things you are talking about are degrees. BSc is a Bachelor of Science, an MSc is a Masters and a PHD is the highest you can get. It means Allan can put doctor in front of his name. God Ger, would you just be QUIET!'

Gerard looked confused. 'Well how was I to know he was still a bachelor, he didn't tell us that, did he? I've got terrible pains in my right foot Allan, would you know what that is?'

Cracker was gradually losing patience with Gerard. 'You'll get my foot up yer fuckin arse so ye will if ye don't shut yer'

Siobhan raised her hand and told them to calm down.

'Gerard if you interrupt again I will have to ask you to leave the room. You know how to listen, so just listen please.'

Gerard looked at the floor, embarrassed and murmured.

'Okay so.'

'Where was I?' Allan said.

'Harvard.' Ant reminded him.

'I was lucky there; I had a professor who mentored me. One of his previous pupils was Vice President in Mortgage Backed Securities Research at Smith Barney. Every holiday, and any spare time I had, I would go there. I have a passion for analysis. In fact it's an obsession, I analyze everything. I also have an obsession with finance and world affairs

'When I finished my PHD I wanted to come back to Ireland. I was offered a job in the biggest financial institution here, as a research analyst. I was promoted pretty quickly to portfolio manager. I'm a consultant working in high finance.'

Allan took his time, poured himself a glass of water and swallowed it in one go. The men were watching him silently, completely fascinated by him, with the exception of Cracker. Arms folded Cracker sat straight in his chair.

'What the fuck is a fellah like him sitting here for?' he thought. 'Maybe he's going to offer us a job or teach us fucking maths!'

Bins looked at Allan as if he was another species. He has never been up so close to a man like him. The nearest he had ever been to one, was either his lawyer or his probation officer.

Allan continued. 'One evening soon after I returned to Ireland, my father told me he wanted to talk to me…..'

He paused and ran his hands through his blonde hair. His then clasped his hands together so tightly, the skin of each finger appeared translucent across his knuckles. His demeanor changed from the confident, calm person he had projected ten seconds before, to one of uncertainty. He frowned, looked at men and said in a whisper 'that was the day, my life and my world as I knew it, fell apart!'

Allan looked at Siobhan as if he wasn't quite sure if he wanted to continue or not. After a few seconds he stood up, slipped his hands into his trouser pockets and started pacing around the room. His Ralph Lauren chinos moved soundlessly on the carpet.

Except for Gerard the men kept their eyes fixed firmly on Siobhan. They were unsure if they should turn and look at Allan's movements or to look straight ahead.

Siobhan held their attention until Allan started to speak again.

'I'm sorry but this is a bit nerve-racking for me, Siobhan's the only person apart from my father who knows what really happened to me. When I'm nervous I have to walk about, so if you don't mind I will just keep walking until I can sit down again.'

'Do whatever makes you feel comfortable Allan,' said Ant.

'My father told me that he was proud of me and my achievements, and a few other things, and assured me of the strong and loving relationship we have. He said he couldn't wish for a better son. Then he looked me straight in the eyes, and told me I wasn't his biological son! That was the first shock but the worst was yet to come.

'He asked me if I remembered anything about my life before I had come to live with him.

'I told him I didn't remember much. I had short flashbacks of shouting, pain and bad feelings in my stomach. I also remembered hitting my head a lot, but that was about all.'

Siobhan watched Allan move around the floor; all the men were concentrating on Allan, their eyes moving in the motion of watching a tennis match.

She hesitated when she saw the expression on Dezzie's face.

'Okay so far,' she thought, 'please God don't let him slip into his blank space.'

Allan continued.

'My father told me about the day he took me away from my mother.'

'The day you came here son, I'd had a frantic call from your mother, shouting and screaming down the phone. I couldn't understand a word she said except that you were hurt. I drove as fast as I could to her house, when I arrived you were lying on the floor in the sitting room, covered in blood. Your mouth was bleeding, your little face was black with bruises and your underpants were soaked in blood.'

Dezzie winced. He automatically started to draw his legs up but stopped as he saw Siobhan frowning at him. Siobhan sat straighter in her chair breathing in slowly looking into his eyes. Dezzie mimicked her posture.

'There wasn't a sound from you Allan, my father said, "you just lay there. I wrapped you in a blanket and ran with you to my car, all the time she was shouting and screaming rubbish about your uncle and herself.

'All I could understand was your uncle had been there; she kept shouting, "nothing happened, nothing happened. He just fell."

'No mobile phones in those days, I had to leave you in the car and rush back into her house and phone a surgeon friend of mine, telling him to meet me at my house."'

'I told my father I couldn't remember any of this.'

'Thank God for that,' he said.

Allan seemed to feel more relaxed; he stopped walking and sat in his chair. Crossing his legs he placed one hand over the other and rested them on his lap. He bowed his head and slowly looked up, his eyes fixed first on Bins, then on Tom's and the others. Except for Cracker not one of them held Allan's gaze.

Dezzie looked at Siobhan, she returned his look, nodding gently as if to say 'it's okay Dezzie, you are safe.'

Allan's voice became a whisper. 'I had been cold-bloodedly and systematically tortured by those two sadists from the time my father had left my mother. I had been assaulted in the most grotesque, way by my own family!'

Ant said, 'Jesus Christ, the bastard devils. Its beyond belief human-beings could do that to an infant!'

214

The tears started to roll down Gerard's face and he wiped them away with the cuff of his sleeve, the room felt has though a blanket had been thrown over it.

'My father went on to explain about the memories I had of knocking my head.'

'There are many things I discovered Allan. When your uncle visited, your mother she kept you tied half-naked to the leg of a chair.

'She put you under the table sitting on a potty. Every time you tried to get up, you hit your head on the table!

'My friend couldn't believe the injuries the two of them had inflicted on you that day. He decided we would take you to a small private hospital, outside Dublin.

'You see the problem was now about damage control. Of course your safety was our primary concern, but we also realized if a journalist got hold of this, we all, including you for the rest of your life, would carry an infamous label and legacy.

'It was while you were in the hospital I discovered you were not my son. I have an extremely rare blood type AB-Rh Negative, yours is O+ the same as your mother!'

Allan paused to let this information sink in and give the men time to assimilate it.

'Christ!' said Bins interrupting Allan. 'And to think we thought we had it bad. At least we were damaged by shaggin strangers, Jayzus shaggin Christ!'

Dezzie stood up and walked over to Allan, he put his hand on Allan's shoulder.

'I'm sorry Allan; I don't know how you've come through all of that, when I think how I've wasted half my life feeling sorry for myself.......'

Siobhan interrupted.

'As I have said before gentlemen, there is no comparison with personal pain. There is no degree of less or more. We all own and feel our pain in a different way.'

The men were quiet. The atmosphere had changed in the room. Cracker thought 'Christ his own fucking mother, fucking, dirty, mad bitch!'

'Allan,' said Ant. 'What happened to your mother?'

'I never saw her from the day my father took me Ant. My father explained that he gave her a choice; stay in Ireland or England and he would have her and her brother put in prison. On the proviso that she never contacted me again my father gave her a lump sum and a large monthly allowance.

'He told me all of this because when I was at Harvard he had news that she had died of a brain tumor. He didn't want to tell me but he wanted me to know and be able to understand, why I felt the way I did sometimes. He didn't want to hold onto a secret that was partially mine. He believed I had the right to know my own history. My father also felt that secrets have a way of being exposed when you least expect. By knowing my background I would always be prepared for exposure.'

'Your father was a wise man Allan, you were l… lucky to have his strength and p… protection. Is he still alive?' Tom asked.

'He is thank God. He's retired of course and lives abroad, but I spend a lot of time with him.'

Gerard puts up his hand, like a child wishing to speak.

'Yes Gerard,' Allan said patiently.

'Well I don't know if I am out of order Allan, and you don't have to answer me if you don't want to…. but, did you ever find out who was your real father?'

Allan looked at Siobhan questioningly; she nodded her head and raised her forehead slightly.

'It is entirely up to you Allan,' she said.

Allan smoothed out an imaginary crease in his trousers, ran his fingers through his hair and took a deep breath.

'I did Gerard,' Allan said quietly, looking down at his shoes. Cracker cracked his knuckles. Tom winced again at the sound. Dezzie shifted in his seat and hugged his knees, the others held their breath.

'It was my uncle.'

'Jayzus Christ!' Bins said, looking behind himself.

'Jaysus what kind of shaggin people were they at all?'

'Worser than fuckin animals,' said Cracker, 'I'd have fucking swung for the bastard s.'

Dezzie got up from his chair quickly and ran for the garden door. Once outside, the others could hear him retching. Ant reacted instantly and carried a glass of water outside to him.

'It's okay Dezzie, you're okay man, let it out and you'll be fine. That's it now, take a deep breath.' he said, his hand gently patting Dezzie's back.

After a minute the two of them came back into the room, Dezzie looked pale but smiled. 'Sorry lads, I don't know what happened to me, sorry about that.'

'Sher y… alright there Dezzi me lad, th… think nothing o-o-of it, said Tom.'

Allan sat calmly in his chair and looked with sympathy at the men who were trying so hard to support him and each other. Men who had never met each other until a few hours before.

'There's one more thing I have to tell you all,' he said.

'My uncle's name was, McGowan!'

Chapter 11

THE SILENT shock reverberated around the room like electricity. Siobhan looked at them, scanning their faces and their body language. Cracker took her attention.

Cracker flexed every muscle in his body, the veins in his neck expanded and protruded like small twigs. His eyes were like slits, his lips closed in on his teeth. Then the snarl came rising from his stomach, increasing in volume 'till it came it came out in a scream of agony.

Tom jumped from his seat and with one leap ran behind Siobhan. Dezzie curled into the fetal position with his hands over his ears. Gerard sat rigid, blinking as if he was going to be attacked. Ant moved in front of Cracker and without touching him, tried to soothe him.

'It's okay Cracker, it's okay, you're in a safe place, it's okay.'

Siobhan walked slowly towards Cracker, his eyes were staring at her, but they were blank.

'Cracker,' she said softly, 'he can't touch you, no one can touch you.'

She held out her hand to him and he took it. Gently, like a child holding onto his mother she led him out of the back door into the garden. Turning to the others she motioned with her hand for them to sit down.

'Do your breathing all of you.'

Once outside she let go of Cracker's hand and steered him towards a chair. He sat down heavily. Siobhan held her diamond pendant in front of Cracker's heavily glazed eyes.

His eyes involuntarily twitched then focused on the pendant.

'Think of your revenge Cracker,' she whispered to him.

'Your time is coming. You are not alone any more Cracker, the time has almost come. When I say three, two, one Cracker, you will find yourself in the garden with me. You will forget all the bad feelings you have right now. Three, two, one.'

Cracker slowly looked around the garden, 'It's lovely here isn't it Siobhan, very peaceful?'

'It is Cracker and it's a beautiful evening, shall we go inside now and join the others?'

'Whatever you say Siobhan, lead the way and we'll play follow my leader.'

The men looked relaxed, with the exception of Allan who looked nervously at Siobhan. Gerard seemingly had taken control of the situation and had become the unelected therapist.

'How are yes lads?' Cracker said enthusiastically. 'Shove up yer arse there Gerard, and give me a seat.'

Gerard looked at Cracker and then at Siobhan, she nodded to him and smiled. Gerard did as he was asked.

'Now we've all been doing our breathing and self' hpnototics Siobhan and we're grand, aren't we lads. Were great so we are,' said Bins.

'Did ye have a good holiday Cracker me lad?' Cracker looked at Bins as if he was a lunatic and ignored him.

'I'm sorry if I caused a problem,' said Allan, as he looked first at Siobhan then at the others.

Cracker looked at him, 'sher maybe none of us woulda had a fuckin problem if yer fuckin judgy daddy had had the balls to do something about his prick of a brother-in-law, when he found out about him.'

'It wasn't as easy as that Cracker,' said Allan, 'and don't forget that McGowan wasn't the only one. Look how many of them there are being investigated right now?'

Cracker ignored him. 'Ah well he said, sher he'll get what's coming to him soon enough, as I said he'll get what's coming to him.'

'Well' said Dezzie looking at Allan, 'I don't know how you survived that, Jesus, I thought I had it bad.'

'Ah sher didn't we all have our shaggin lives ruined by it all, anywayaz, I suppose we are lucky to be here to tell the tale.'

Allan looked around the room, his heart went out to the men he had spent the evening with, an evening he knew he would remember for the rest of his life. Each one of them in their own way a hero.

It was now Siobhan's time to talk. 'As I said in the beginning gentlemen, there is no measurement for pain in this room.

'You have all suffered indescribable events as very young children and then into adolescence.

'Each one of you has had the tremendous courage to come here and face your demons every week. You've changed from victims to survivors and are moving on with your lives. A round of applause for all of you and thank you for coming tonight.'

Siobhan started clapping and the men joined in, smiling and patting each other on the back.

Siobhan turned her pendant showing the diamond side.

'I think it might be a good idea if we do a little relaxation before you all leave, what do you think?'

'I'm sorry,' said Allan but I will have to leave you all now, unfortunately I have an appointment. It has been a pleasure to meet you all and I hope we can meet again in the near future.'

They all jumped up to shake Allan's hand and told him how much they'd enjoyed meeting him.

'Now Allan me lad,' said Gerard, 'if there's anyting you need, anyting at all just give me a bell.'

Allan smiled at Gerard. 'I will and thank you all again.'

Siobhan accompanied Allan to the door.

'You know Siobhan,' he said to her, 'You are a very special lady, I don't think you know just how special you are.'

Siobhan thanked him and told him she would see him next week.

When she returned to the room the men were preparing themselves for their relaxation.

Bins jumped onto the floor and resumed his position after looking behind him, then he decided to pull his shoes off.

Gerard had already started exhaling loudly; Cracker sat up straight with a slight smile on his face.

Dezzie didn't try to get into the fetal position; he sat comfortably with his hands relaxed on the arms of the chair. Ant stroked his beard relaxed and smiled. Tom sat back with his hands relaxed on his knees.

They all looked at Siobhan for a second and closed their eyes.

The only sound in the room was gentle breathing and Siobhan's voice which was so low it was hardly audible.

'Three, two, one. Take your time now; when you are ready open your eyes,' she said.

The men stretched their bodies and smiled at each other.

'Well I don't know about you lads,' said Gerard, 'but I feel feckin great. Are we comin again to the group next week Siobhan?'

Siobhan looked at them all and smiled.

'If you would like to continue now you have bonded with each other, I think you will get a lot out of it.'

'Well I fer one am in, how about youze lads?'

They agreed that they wouldn't miss it for the world, they would be very happy to come again.

One by one they said good night to Siobhan, thanking her and reluctantly moved towards the door.

They filed out into the cool evening air and formed a group, talking, laughing and patting each other on the back or the shoulder. Even Cracker, who loathed anyone touching him, was holding onto Tom's hand as if he didn't want to let go.

As she watched them Siobhan had a mental image of six little boys. They were walking down a road with their arms around each other's shoulders in comradeship. They were wearing the old uniforms of the institutions. Socks hanging down, big boots, knee length trousers held up by braces; and shirts with the odd sleeve rolled up. Their hair was short and shaved up the back of their neck.

'It worked,' she said to herself. Now they really are survivors. Tonight they learned they were not alone, they can feel what the words friendship and trust mean.

Siobhan listened for a while to the murmurs and laughter outside, and then she walked into the garden and stood in front of the tree of reconciliation and inner tranquility.

She smiled to herself, her mind at peace.

Chapter 12

THE NIGHT was cold and dark. Typical of the Emerald Isle weather, one minute everyone congratulating themselves that they'd never seen the sun shine as bright and taking personal credit for it. The next berating anyone who would listen that nuclear fallout and cheap Chinese labour was responsible for weather that even a polar bear wouldn't venture out into it.

Glasnevin graveyard was quiet, as it would be with the places full of dead people.

The dim moon threw ghostly shadows on dark, cold, lonely angels and marble gravestones advertising the date of birth and age at death of the occupants hidden beneath them.

'I shaggin hate graveyards,' said Bins. 'Shaggin waste of space so they are. I'm going to have my body incin, incin, shaggin burnt, so I am. The shaggers can do what they want wid de ashes. Dey can roll them up in a joint and shaggin smoke them for all I care.'

'I'm going to leave my body to science,' said Gerard.

'For focks sake,' whispered Cracker, 'what kinda science want your body?'

'Zoology science,' Gerard replied.

'I'm the one person in the whole of mankind which could prove we came from apes!'

'Will you all be quiet for God's sake,' said Ant.

'Why?' said Bins. 'Who are we goin to shaggin wake up?'

Dezzie pointed out to Tom, he was walking on a grave. Cracker said what difference did it make what you walked on, you were hardly going to walk on anyone's toes or feelings?

'It's just up here a ways,' said Cracker.

Then they saw him. Like a shadow in the shape of an old man, he was sitting on a bench wrapped in a long coat wearing a scarf. No hat, no gloves. Holding his pipe in one hand he was staring into space. It was cold, dark and silent.

Not a sound, except a slight rustle from the see-through plastic suits which covered their clothes from head to foot. Bins had provided the suits courtesy of the garbage municipality. Each of them wore plastic shower caps on their heads, blue Marigold gloves and plastic Tesco bags over their shoes secured by elastic bands.

Cracker led the way, followed by Bins, Dezzie, Gerard, Tom and Ant.

Cracker carried a sawn-off shot gun.

Dezzie carried a Japanese sword he had bought at a car boot sale years ago. Bin's carried a roll of extra strong black plastic bin-bags, courtesy also of the garbage municipality. Tom carried a steak knife. Ant carried a hammer and a wooden stake carved to a point.

The group stopped. 'Ar are you sh… sh… shure now Cracker that's yer m man?'

'Wait 'till ye get up to him Tom,' Cracker replied. 'Ye said y'd never forget the smell of him, an I'm telling ye, yr about to be introduced to it again in a minute.'

'Don't ferget you'se now that his fuckin head is mine!'

'Okay Cracker but I want to cut it off. I'm the warrior,' whispered Dezzie.

'I'll kick the shaggin legs of 'im till they break, there'll be nothing left of them to put in a shaggin wheelbarra,' whispered Bins.

Tom waved his steak knife in the air. 'I'll cut the dick off him. The thing h… he used to m… mur… urder my brother.'

'I'll break his wrists and then I want to push the stake through his devil heart,' said Ant.

Cracker whispered, 'right so, let's get on with it lads.'

They were passed caring about noise now. A steady stream of adrenalin flowed quickly through their veins, their body shut down blocking everything except the anger of revenge.

'How r yez McGowan? De yez remember us?' Cracker taunted the man menacingly. The old man stared straight ahead of him, not saying a word.

'The devil is feckin deaf! So he is,' said Gerard.

Bins looked behind him. 'I don't care if he's shaggin blind as well, let's gerron wid it fer Christ sake, it's shaggin freezing out here.'

Cracker holding the gun by the barrel, walked behind the old man, raising the gun high above his head, he brought the barrel down with such force there was an ear-splitting crack. Simultaneously the back of the old man's head opened something dark slipped out and a gush of blood with the pressure of a geyser sprayed over Bin's plastic suit.

'You messed wid my fuckin head for long enough.'

Cracker lifted the gun again and smashed it down on the pulp that was once a skull.

'How does it feel ye ould focker te have your head messed with?'

Dezzie jumped in front of Cracker.

'Give me a chance, give me a chance Cracker, get outta the way all of you.'

They all took a few steps back.

With one mighty swipe of his sword Dezzie decapitated the old man's head. It fell on the ground. Bins started kicking it around, playing and dribbling with it, as if it were a football. The head disappeared into the darkness. Then in frenzy Bins kicked the old man's legs, there was the constant sound of bones cracking. Exhausted he stood back and surveyed the completion of his revenge.

'Okay Tom there ya are lad, he's all yoers,' Bins said calmly.

Tom tore at the old man's, blood soaked trousers. He ripped open the fly and pulled out the man's penis. Holding it in one hand, the steak knife in the other, he slashed his way through skin and gristle 'till it came free.

Retaining the penis between thumb and forefinger, he held it up, looking at it he blinked.

'Jayzus isn't't it fuh… funny lads, I thought it wouldda been a lot bigger than that, sher it's no b… bigger than me little f… fuh… finger!'

Taking his hammer Ant smashed with rage, accompanied by a frenzy of curses on the old man's hands and wrists. When he finished he threw what was left of the body onto the ground. He tore open the coat, cardigan, shirt and vest exposing the old man's chest. With the stake held in both hands he raised his arms as high as he could, and pounded it into the old man's heart. His rage still not dissipated he picked up the hammer. With two hefty strikes the stake plunged further into the chest. Ant stopped, breathless when he heard the sound of gravel underneath the old man's back. They stood, breathing heavily and looking at each other.

'Jayzus,' said Gerard, 'Look at the state of us, we look as though we have the fekin measles?'

They looked at Gerard, Cracker started to laugh, Tom followed.

Gerard looked at Tom and said. 'Isn't it strange Tom how you don't laugh with a stutter?'

'Isn't it strange Ger how yer shaggin comb-over isn't so noticeable through the shaggin shower cap?' growled Cracker.

They all laughed.

'Jayzus,' said Gerard, 'that was more fun than a fekin hurling match.'

'Right,' said Bins, 'that's it so. Get over to that pipe there, hose yerselves down. Take off the plastic suits and put them in this bin bag, I'll take care of the rest.'

Chapter 13

DETECTIVE MARK Quinn headed up the investigation into the 'Graveyard Slaughter.' The whole country had been shocked at the violence and brutality of the murder of an old man in the graveyard.

At first investigators considered it a ritualistic killing. The stake through the heart of what was left of the victim was Draconian. The decapitation, destruction of limbs and hacking off the penis; was considered over-kill, it was considered atrocious, relentless and merciless. The primary evidence they had so far, pointed to a perpetrator of huge strength who was no doubt psychotic.

Discovering the victim was a member of a religious organisation led them to the head office of the Christian Brothers. Mark himself had poured over the ancient annals which contained sweet as honey, biographical details of every retired or deceased member of an association, the members of which, had one thing in common, their interest in children!

Garda data-base disclosed information that several complaints of sexual abuse against the deceased over the past few years had been filed, but either not followed up, or if they had been investigated no further action had been taken.

Each man they had interviewed led to another man, everyone knew someone who held a grudge against McGowan. From the information they had accumulated so far, the consensus between the men working on the case was 'the old bastard deserved what he got.'

An unusual amount of suspects were receiving therapeutic intervention by mental health providers. Practitioners were interviewed and more and more information was gleaned.

Mark had personally interviewed Siobhan.

A divorcee of more than ten years, Mark had little interest in women, one experience was enough. His job entailed long hours which were not conducive to family life.

Arriving home unexpectedly and finding his wife in an outstandingly, and bewildering skilful, sexual contortion with one of his colleagues; had undermined his confidence in himself and his occupational role as a detective.

If he didn't have the ability to discover the existence of another man in his bed for two years, he wondered what the hell he was doing in his current position within the frame of criminality.

His confusion was undermined even more that Mark was considered a more than average attractive man; whilst the colleague enjoying his ex-wife's sexual gymnastics was considered to be one point up on the scale of being repulsive. There had been a few liaisons in the intervening years; however he had issues with trust. He also imagined that most of the women he had entertained over short periods had their eye on his house and pocket more than on him. For the time being he was content with his non-marital and uninvolved status. That was up until he met Siobhan.

Mark had seen Siobhan being interviewed on a television program more than a year ago. Preparing an evening meal for himself he was more involved with his noodles as he listened to the program more than viewing it. Nothing prepared him for the physical reaction he experienced when Siobhan opened the door to him on his first visit to her consulting rooms. She was stunning, 'what the hell was she doing working in this profession?' he thought.

One hour later, he said goodbye, she closed the door behind him, and he sat in his unmarked car wondering where the ignition was! 'My God,' he said to himself, 'it isn't just her looks it's her presence, there's a magic to her, I feel as though I am in a different space.'

When Mark had telephoned her for an appointment to see her again, with regard to the 'Graveyard Slaughter,' she had apologized; she had very little time, and gave him an appointment for the end of the week.

'I'm sorry to disturb you again Siobhan. There is just a little more information I hoped you might be able to give me.'

Siobhan invited him to sit down and he sat opposite her. She was calm and relaxed; as she had been the first time they met. His feelings of warmth, excitement and attraction surfaced once more. As she crossed one slender leg over the other he had to stop the compulsion he felt, to just sit and stare at her, rather than talk.

Siobhan could feel the chemistry between them. It was a vibrant flow of energy, however she knew how to push it down and suppress it. Siobhan would rather plunge into the icy waters of the Antarctic than into an intimate relationship.

'Well I don't see how I can help you any more with your enquiries Detective Quinn.'

'Mark,' he said, 'please call me Mark, Siobhan.'

Siobhan nodded her head.

'Okay, Mark, it is.'

'Well so far Siobhan,' he said, 'we've interviewed hundreds of men. Some have alibi's others don't. The main consensus between the lot of them was, they either didn't remember the victim, or thought the bastard deserved everything he got!'

Siobhan remained silent and passive; he had never known a woman who could look directly into his eyes for a long time and comfortly retain contact. He was becoming nervous, he wanted a response from her, any response, another smile would do.

He realized he had made a statement, he hadn't asked her a question, therefore why did he expect a response? He continued.

'It is quite apparent from our investigations that the victim was a profoundly immoral man for many years of his life. I might even say he was sadistic to the point of being evil.' There was still no verbal response from Siobhan.

'There are a good few who have a motive for annihilating him, but not one in particular who would have the strength, at their age, to carry out the violence perpetrated on the victim. Six of those men have a motive and well deserved motives, however they all have alibi's. The six of them are all your clients,' he said.

Siobhan still held eye contact with Mark; she was looking at him intensely, as if every word he said was the most interesting thing she had ever heard.

Mark continued, 'They were all here in a Group when the event took place, and they say you can confirm that?'

There was silence....

'And,' said Siobhan, as if she was waiting for a response from him.

'Well' Mark said, 'Can you confirm that?'

'I can tell you Mark that each week, I run three therapeutic groups. In order for me to give you any information about them or the participants I have to have their written permission. I think you are aware of that.'

'Yes I am Siobhan, which is why I have brought their written consent with me.'

Mark took an envelope from his pocket it and opened it; he handed over six sheets of paper, all neatly folded. Siobhan took them and opened them. He noticed how slim her fingers were the nails unadorned with nail polish appearing as though she had the perfect French manicure.

He watched her read through the few lines on each paper. All of them had the same statement. Each document was signed by a participant and dated.

Siobhan read carefully through each document and noted the signatures of each of her gentlemen.

'May I keep these Mark please?'

'Of course Siobhan.'

'Yes,' she replied, 'I can confirm that these gentlemen were present in group therapy that evening.'

Siobhan smiled at him, he felt as if he had been given a pot of gold and all she had given him was a simple affirmative.

'Thank you Siobhan.'

'You are welcome Mark.'

'That's a beautiful pendant you're wearing Siobhan.'

Siobhan fingering the pendant thanked him.

'I read an article somewhere about Spiral Hypnosis, could your pendant be used be used for that procedure Siobhan? It is a spiral isnt it?'

'I suppose it could Mark.'

'You use hypnosis in your work, don't you Siobhan?'

'When it's relevant I do, yes.'

'May I ask you when it would be relevant?' Mark enquired.

'I work with victims of trauma Mark. I am not sure you would understand the significance of hypnosis, or even the psychological terminology!'

'Well perhaps you can explain it to me in a simple way Siobhan, that's if you have the time?'

Siobhan looked at her watch. Mark noticed it was a simple Rolex, no diamonds just plain white gold, fashionable but not flashy. There was nothing flashy about the woman in front of him; she was the epitome of grace and elegance.

'I have the time Mark, school is out for the weekend and even the teachers are allowed to play.'

Mark hadn't noticed it was Friday. Every day seemed the same to him. When he wasn't working, he was thinking about work.

'My treatment is tailored to the needs of each and every person who walks through that door. It is a long and painful process for all of them. It is a phased framework consisting of stabilization, trauma processing, and integration. Hypnotic techniques are mostly used for stabilization and grounding. I do not agree with, or use hypnosis to recover memories.'

Mark said: 'Is it possible to hypnotize someone to uncover if they have committed a crime?'

'There is no scientific evidence to prove any recovered memory can be reliable. To retrieve a memory intact, first of all the patient would have to be asked a certain question. Just asking the question, would be, in fact an auto suggestion!' Siobhan looked at Mark to ascertain if he was following her explanation.

'I see,' he said.

'So if I said to one of the six in your group, for instance, after he had been hypnotized, "were you one of the men in the graveyard?" That would be an auto-suggestion?'

'Yes it would, therefore it would pollute or nullify his response,' Siobhan replied.

'If you were looking at it from the legal point of view Mark, it would never stand up in a court of law. Apart from the obvious fact that no one would agree to hypnosis if they thought for a minute they were going to implicate themselves in a crime.

'No court could order a person to be hypnotized, or give evidence under hypnosis; it would violate any and every established moral principle. It would also be a breach of Human Rights.'

'Yes of course Siobhan I know very well it would be immoral. I was simply asking the question to further my knowledge about the subject as I know little about it.'

Siobhan smiled at him, he smiled back.

'You were a victim of the institutions. Weren't you Siobhan?'

'So,' thought Siobhan, he's not only investigating the clients, he's probably investigating every one that plays a role in their lives. She was not shocked, she wasn't particularly concerned. Her background was not public knowledge; it was her business and no one else's. Siobhan had, had two clients who had been murdered and one who had committed murder. After working briefly at Rikers Island she knew very well the implications of being their therapist. Her work was confidential, only a court-order could force her to reveal any information about a client, without that client's written permission.

However, it was her personal choice to either answer Mark's question or tell him it was none of his business.

'Mark, you do understand, I have allowed you into my work-place, which is a confidential space?'

'Oh, I know, I'm sorry Siobhan, perhaps it was impolite of me to ask that question, I apologie, you don't have to answer it.'

'Damn' he said to himself, 'why did I find the necessity to ask that bloody question, now she'll throw me out.'

'Yes Mark, I was in Goldenbridge,' Siobhan replied.

Mark realized he had been holding his breath, he felt anxious and nervous. Sometimes he hated his job and this was one of those times. He didn't want to continue, but he had to know as much about this woman as he could. He knew deep down he was looking for a flaw, there could be no diamond which was flawless. Perhaps if he could find a hint of something negative about her, the feelings which were growing within him would subside.

He found himself following her tone of voice. His voice became quieter, his face softer. He wondered if she could hypnotize him without him realizing. He was doing so much self-talk he was getting on his own nerves.

'You had a younger sister didn't you? What was her name now, was it Mary?'

'Yes it was Mary.'

Mark knew the answers to the questions. What he didn't know, was how to proceed with asking them.

He had no communication-skills which would allow dialogue between him and this woman.

'She died in there Siobhan, didn't she, what age was she?'

Siobhan presented the same calm exterior. It had taken years working through her childhood experiences, and the shadowy memories which used to emerge from the past. Had she not had the ability and courage to exorcise her own demons, how could she possibly help and guide others through the process.

'Mary was six, when she died.'

'How old were you at that time Siobhan?'

'I was eight Mark.'

There was silence for moment both of them looking at each.

'How did Mary die Siobhan?'

'They said she fell out of a window!'

'It must have been terrible for you Siobhan?'

'Yes it was Mark. I stopped speaking for months, I either couldn't or didn't want to speak. Of course nobody cared if I spoke or not. No one cared if I was dead or alive. One day there were a lot of visitors. Everything changed if there were visitors. Lovely food on the tables, toys put around the place. Lovely bed spreads on the beds, everything changed overnight and by the next day everything disappeared again.

'Among the visitors were a man and woman who were lovely. They talked to me but I couldn't talk back. They adopted me and took me to England. My adopted father was a GP and my mother was a psychiatrist. I was their only child. From the day they took me out of that place, I don't think I had one unhappy moment. I was very lucky Mark.'

Siobhan recognized an expression which passed over Mark's face for less than a second. Communication isn't simply by words, she thought. Sometimes language isn't enough. Sometimes it is too much. What can you say when you are holding the hand of a dying child? A recognition of a previous existence passed between them.

Mark waited for the moment to pass.

'Can I ask your opinion on something Siobhan?'

'I rarely give my opinion Mark. Opinions are simply thoughts, feelings and a certain amount of knowledge expounded most of the time, by those who don't have enough knowledge on the subject.'

'Yes,' he replied, 'but I've seen you being interviewed on the television as an expert in your field and every wants to listen to your opinion.'

'Mark, it isn't that easy.'

Her voice was like velvet to him, he could sit listening to it all night.

'I have the piece of paper which stipulates I am an expert in that field. What is the highest grade one can reach at any academic level? What is the relationship between expert knowledge and exceptional performance in a certain field?'

Mark was becoming confused; he wished he hadn't asked the question.

'Academia Mark is not actually a benchmark for experience, especially in my field. For instance; is a woman with a PHD in Post Traumatic Stress Disorder, more knowledgeable than a nurse with a primary degree, but she is working with the Red Cross, covering natural and man-made disasters? There is no comparison is there Mark?

'I do not consider myself an expert in any given subject. I consider I have expertise in that subject. No one can know everything there is to know about any subject,' said Siobhan.

'I understand Siobhan, so let me put it this way then. What is your impression of those religious institutions Siobhan, after all you work with a lot of the survivors?'

'They were not religious institutions Mark,' Siobhan, her voice as soft as velvet, her facial expression calm without so much as a frown. It was as if she was talking about a walk in the park. Mark felt as though he was in another space without walls or anything tangible. Siobhan continued.

'Neither were they institutions for the religious. They were the spawning grounds for the devil's minions.

'They were financed by the church or wealthy philanthropists either trying to buy their way into heaven, or, buy their way out of hell. These devil worshippers had an endless supply of innocents to perfect their trade on.

They burned the image of the cross they wore like an anvil around their neck, into the imagination of each and every child who entered through their doors.

A cross with the image of a man agonized in the last throes of a torturous death. An ornament which signified the very heart of Christianity.

'They blamed the child for that man's suffering by constantly telling him, "Look he died for you, because of your sins!"

'Thousands of children, down through four generations, grew into adults who believed they were bad, believed they were evil.'

Mark realized he was holding his breath, he didn't want to move in case he interrupted the flow and obviously passionate analysis of this woman's impression of institutional abuse.

'This,' Siobhan continued, 'was a group of male and female psychopathic sadists and pedophiles.

'The Parish Priests knew about it. The Bishops knew about it. The Archbishops knew about it. The Papal Nuncio knew about it, and I'm as sure as hell the Pope knew about it!

'This was Holy Catholic Ireland, Mark, with Holy Catholic Children. Not the German Third Reich abusing and murdering Jewish children.

'These criminals didn't just take away the children's childhood, they took away their future. In the majority of cases they destroyed their children's future and their children's children future.

'There was a culture of conspiracy which reached the highest level. It thrived on the same secrecy as a cult. When, and I mean rarely when it occurred that a victim was listened to, he or she might have been financially compensated. However not only was the victim sworn to secrecy but also the priest or Bishop who dealt with the case. Did you know those people had to swear an oath of secrecy with regard to these cases? If they broke the oath they would and were defrocked.

'Unfortunately Mark the majority of people do not understand the difference between truth and speculation.

'The truth is Mark. Rome covered up wholesale child abuse. For more than one generation and not only in Ireland. We are not just talking about the Institutions. My clients range from the age of twenty six to over eighty years of age. We are looking at the years from at least 1928 to today. Look at the likes of Brendan Smith. Look at O'Grady he abused hundreds of children in America.

'The Bishops had the power to protect children from any form of abuse, so ask yourself the question; 'why did they not use their powers.'

All the time Siobhan had been speaking she didn't raise her voice, Mark sat quietly, spellbound and captivated by her.

'You know Mark, there are also the silent victims, whom perhaps people don't know about, or consider. The invisible ones who were locked up in mental hospitals for years. The women in the Magdalene Laundries. The victims who committed suicide, the ones who are still lost in the oblivion of substance abuse, the ones who are in prison and how many of them are there who are still too ashamed to come forward?'

Siobhan stopped speaking; she knew she could speak on this subject for six months without repeating herself, but she didn't feel the necessity to judge, give her opinion or anything other than information.

'Thank you for your time Siobhan and your patience, the picture looks a lot clearer to me now,' Mark said.

'You are welcome Mark,' Siobhan smiled and stood up to show him to the door.

Mark rose slowly from his chair, he looked at her.

'Seeing this is a confidential space, we are in Siobhan, I can reveal to you now: This is no longer a murder investigation. The forensics came back yesterday and it seemed the poor bastard had already been dead for a couple of hours when the perpetrator or perpetrators, Siobhan, tore him to pieces.'

'Oh,' Siobhan said.

'Ah well that's life! Or death,' said Mark.

'What was the cause of death Mark? A heart attack?'

'We are still not quite sure Siobhan. The old man was a diabetic, yet, under one of his finger nails there was a substantial amount of chocolate. The forensic examiner also found a microscopic trace of Polonium-210.'

'You mean the poison used to kill Alexander Litvineko?'

'Yes said Mark. They are not even going to bother to follow that one up. Investigations on the PO-210 are enormously expensive. It's hardly likely the KGB wanted to assassinate him, is it Siobhan?' Mark said with a smile.

Siobhan nodded her head and returned his smile.

Opening the door for him, he turned and faced her.

'You're a beautiful woman Siobhan; would you do me the honor of having dinner with me one evening?'

'I'm sorry Mark it would be unethical for me to date a client.'

Mark frowned. 'I'm not your client Siobhan!'

'You will be Mark. We all have the scars in our eyes. Which one were you in? Artane, or was it Letterfrack?'

Standing with her back to the door after Mark left. Siobhan looked up, her eyes moist with tears, she whispered: 'Ah well my little Mary, talk about the Luck of the Irish.'

Only we could kill a dead man!

Never mind we'll do better next time, this was only a trial run after all.

Chapter 14

SIOBHAN LISTENED to the group of men laughing outside. 'Anyone would think they were brother's, she thought to herself. Well I suppose they fit the category of Blood Brothers!'

Dezzie was the first in the door, followed by Gerard; they greeted her heartily, as if they hadn't a care in the world. Ant wished her a good evening. Cracker beamed at her.

'How are ye Siobhan?'

'I'm very well thank you Cracker,' she replied. Tom, his Arsenal scarf wrapped loosely around his neck smiled at her.

'How a… are you s Siobhan?'

'Very well, and you Tom?'

'I'm great t thanks Siobhan.'

Last but not least Bins entered the room. Speaking through his nose he asked Siobhan how she was, and then looked behind him.

'Well,' Siobhan said as she smiled at them. 'You all look very well tonight. Who would like to start?'

'Ah,' said Dezzie, 'will we not wait for Allan?'

'Allan won't be here this evening gentlemen,'

Siobhan told them.

'Okay, who would like to start?'

Gerard and Ant said simultaneously, 'I would.'

'Whoa. Hold on a minute. You know only one of you can speak at a time,' Siobhan reminded them.

Ant said, 'Well I said it first and I really have something important to say.'

'Okay, Ant go ahead,' Siobhan encouraged him.

Ant pulled a letter out of his pocket, stroked his beard, and looked around at all of them.

Within a second they all took similar envelopes out of their pockets.

'Jayzus,' said Gerard, 'what are we playin here, Snap, or Pass the Fekin Parcel?'

Siobhan couldn't quite grasp what was going on as they compared letters. Ant thrust his letter at her, shouting at the others to be quiet until she had a chance to read it.

'As she read the contents she started to smile, her smile became broader and broader until she laughed out loud.

'Are all your letters the same?'

'Yes they shouted.'

'Oh my goodness, this is unbelievable, well not really, but I am so happy for all of you.'

Dezzie then spoke.

'Siobhan can we do one of those group-hug things they do on the television.'

'Why not,' she said, 'You don't have to do it if you don't want to,' she said looking at all of them. They all jumped up and stretched their arms out; it was a bit like a rugby scrum. Cracker was furious with himself for not positioning himself nearer to Siobhan, Bins and Dezzie had jumped in first, both of them with one arm around her waist, Dezzie inhaling the scent of her Angel perfume.

She clapped her hands and jumped up and down like a child.

'I can't believe it, I am so happy for all of you. You all deserve it. Tom let me have a look at your letter.'

<u>Attention of Mr. Thomas McMahon.</u>

Dear Mr. McMahon

We are the solicitors acting on behalf of the Caolan Trust. We are writing to advise you, you are the beneficiary of a one off payment of £500,000.

This sum will be deposited and invested for you for the period of one year, during which time we will guarantee a minimum of fifty per cent profit. It will then be your decision to inform us if you would like to continue investing any part of it or the whole sum.

We also enclose a Bankers Draft for the sum of £50,000 sterling to be cashed and used at your own personal discretion.

Should you need confirmation of the above please telephone our office.

Yours sincerely

Mr. Stephen Joseph.

'It's unbelievable isn't it Siobhan?' Ant said.

'I thought it was a scam like those African, Jumba Lumbas write on those emails. But I rang Stephen Joseph and it is absolutely genuine. I got my bankers draft the other day, but I don't know what to do with it!'

'C… Chrissie rang that man as well. She w… wet herself with the ex… excitement of it all,' said Tom, 'and we don't even have a b… bank account!'

'Sure I put mine in the Credit Union,' shouted Gerard, 'they took the few bob I owed them. Jayzus now I don't know what to do either. I'm not used to having more than €20 in me pocket and I can't fekin sleep thinking about it.'

Gerard's teeth slipped, he adjusted them with his thumb.

'Anywayas the foirst thing I'm going to do is get me self a new jacket from the Oxfam shop.'

'Well I tell ya lads,' Bins interrupted and looked behind him.

'The best ting ta do, is ta jump on one of dem shaggin cruise boats, to a hot country, relax and tink abouh it.'

'Why did we all get it Siobhan?' Dezzie asked her.

'Who do you think these people are, this Trust? What is a Trust thing anyway Siobhan?'

'A charitable trust is either an organization or a person who donates money to those in need,' Siobhan replied.

'Well how did they fuckin know about us then?' asked Cracker.

'Did ye know them Siobhan? I mean how did they fuckin know about the six of us, or are they given money away all over the place?'

'I have no idea who they are Cracker, or why they gave the money to the six of you' Siobhan replied.

'Well I fuckin rang yer man too, and he told me the only thing he knew, was that it was a filanthrowpissed obviously, but he had no further information. What the fuck is a filanthrowpissed?' asked Cracker.

'A philanthropist,' said Siobhan, 'is a special human being. He/She/They, have a general love of mankind. They have an extraordinary desire to improve the lives of those far less fortunate than themselves. Philanthropist's usually have money, a lot of it, and they form a charitable trust, deposit money into it, which they can then donate, finance or support in one form or another to those they believe deserve it.

'It seems to me the person who has so lovingly and generously given the money to all of you, has no wish for you to know who he is. To me this is the righteous philanthropist. He doesn't desire any recognition or gratitude from the beneficiaries. He does it from his heart, not for any personal gain whatsoever.'

'Well I for one would like to thank him,' said Dezzie. They all agreed they would like to do the same.

Siobhan looked at all of them.

'Treat the money with respect, be careful and take advice, though I think it has been well invested for you already, obviously this person has your welfare very much at heart.

'Don't think about where it came from, just be thankful it did. The only thing I can tell you is that I believe you all deserve it,' she added.

'Funny old life, isn't it?' said Ant.

'Sher what's the sayin?' Gerard asked.

'What shagging goes round shaggin comes round,' said Bins as looked behind him.

As they were leaving Dezzie asked Siobhan if she had a telephone number for Allan. He was disappointed he hadn't been at the meeting and would like to meet up with him and tell him about their good fortune.

'I'm sorry Dezzie, you know I can't give out information about a client.'

After they left Siobhan went into the garden. Sitting beside the tree of reconciliation and tranquility, she whispered.

'Well done Allan, from Russia with Love.'